NEVER, NOW, OR LATER

SANDRA DEE

ISBN: 978-0-578-98243-4

This paperback edition first published in 2022

Book Cover Design by ebooklaunch.com

This novel's story and characters are fictitious. Certain long-standing institutions, agencies, and public offices are mentioned, but the characters involved are wholly imaginable.

Dedication

To my Angel,

Thank you for birthing me with this creative mind
and for your encouragement and support
throughout the course of my life.

You would be so proud of me.

This one is for you, Momma.

CHAPTER 1

~TANISHA~

"Baby, you ready? Our cab is downstairs."

"Yeah, I just have to grab my toiletries off the sink."

Was I ready to leave Mexico? Truth is, no, I was not. This honeymoon was all I could have asked for. I needed this time away from home. But in a few odd hours, my behind would be right back in the state of Michigan where I belonged. And I had to admit that I did miss my girlfriends. Cameron and I had been married for all of 120 hours, and the feeling was indescribable. Now we were on our way back to our regularly scheduled lives.

"Mr. and Mrs. Lewis, your cab awaits to take you to Los Cabos International."

"Thank you, Antonio," I replied to our trip attendant.

I could not help but to admire my husband as we were escorted to our vehicle. God sent me a loving, five-foot-nine piece of chocolate. Me being vanilla, I would have never imagined myself mixing with the opposite. I remember when Cameron approached me six years ago and I failed to give him the time of day. I had just begun my career with Monroe and Fischer, Inc., a company in downtown Chicago. It was my second day as an intern, and I was struggling to learn the

1

business. Fresh out of Jackson State University, I knew that I had my stuff together. Sadly, I lasted only a month before I was let go. I ran into Cam a few weeks later at Starbucks, and we exchanged numbers. I had no intentions of keeping in touch with him because I knew that I'd be moving back to Michigan soon. But Cameron was persistent, and I was not used to that.

We kept in touch and to my surprise, Cameron's job promoted him and relocated him to Michigan. I could not believe it! That's when my career took off again, right in Michigan, and I was back on my grind. Being a school social worker was not an easy task at all. I could deal with so much in one day that it stressed me the hell out. But I had a passion for kids, even though I wasn't ready to have my own. Cameron and I had remained friends throughout those few years, and whenever we encountered difficult times in our personal lives, it seemed to draw us closer. My friends and family could tell, but for so long, I was in denial. Here we were, six years later, and I was happier than I ever thought I would be. As we sat at the airport waiting for our plane, I decided to call one of my best friends to confirm that she was picking us up.

"Tanisha, of course I am going to pick you and Cam up, girl. Who do you think you're dealing with?"

"Alex, I know. I'm sorry but you know I just had to make sure. We don't want to be stranded."

My girlfriend Alex was a trip. We had been best friends since we were kids.

"Now maybe if it were Naomi picking you up, you would need to be worried. Heaven knows that chick is crazy," she said with a laugh.

She was telling the truth. Naomi was my roommate from college. We spent some of the best times of our lives together during my senior year, when she was just a sopho-more. She became my other best friend very quickly. But there was only one word to sum her up: crazy. I wouldn't trade her or Alex for the world.

"All right, Alex, six o'clock on the dot!"

"Gotcha, girl, now hang up so I can finish cooking my breakfast. Bye!"

This girl hung up on me.

"Babe, you know I love you, right?" Cameron pulled me in closer.

I replied, "Of course, bae."

"I had a real good time with you, and I just want you to know that."

I loved the assurance my love gave me. It made me won-der what God had in store for me next. I hadn't been in too many relationships in my life. Maybe that was a blessing in disguise. I was nowhere near perfect, and of course Cameron knew that. As I grabbed my husband's hand and kissed his luscious lips, I couldn't help but grin on the inside at the love I had found.

CHAPTER 2

~ALEXANDRA~

"Alexandra? Is that you, girl?" I turned around swiftly to see who the heck recognized me at Starbucks.

"Leon?" I gave him a squinty eye and a half grin.

"Yeah, it's me! How you been doing?!"

Out of all the possible people I could run into Lord, you would allow it to be him. Leon and I first met when we were in law school a few years prior, and shortly after I introduced him to my two best friends, he became an acquaintance of ours. But I had been the target of his affection for some time now.

"Oh, I've been doing well, Leon. Up to the same old stuff, I suppose."

"You still look beautiful, my darling."

I looked horrible. It was ten o'clock in the morning, I'd just come from the gym with my hair all frizzed up, probably still dripping in sweat, and he gives me a compliment.

"Thank you. You look nice yourself."

I thought I could break loose when it was my turn to order in line.

Approaching the counter as I turned away from Leon, I asked the cashier, "May I get a medium iced coffee and three blueberry scones please?"

I could tell that Leon was still up for some conversation, but I wasn't feeling it.

"Your total is seven dollars and ninety-one cents, ma'am."

"All right," I replied. I reached for my pocket wallet but I didn't feel it. *Uh oh.* "Uh, it looks like I left my wallet in my car. Can you hold my order until I come back?" The young cashier gave me a smirk like she had a problem. As she proceeded to open her mouth, Leon chimed in.

"I'll take care of it. Here you go, miss. Just add a large Frappuccino to the order please," he said as he handed the cashier his bank card.

I was in no way shocked. "Leon, thank you. I'll pay you back when—"

"No, Alex, you're fine. It's really no problem."

Gosh, now I felt like I owed him a favor.

"Hey, are you in a hurry?" he asked.

I hesitated but then fixed my lips to say, "Umm, not really. You want to sit?"

"Sure," he said.

I figured I'd just talk to him briefly. When we sat, I noticed that something was different about him. I knew it had been a minute since I'd seen him, but what was different?

"So, I take it you're still single?"

Of course he would break the ice with the main thing he was curious to know.

"Yes, I am still single."

"And how is that working out for you?" he asked.

"I have to admit that it's working out in my favor."

I guess he expected a different response.

"Well, that's good to know. It's kind of a shock to me since you still look this good after two years."

"Leon, did you expect me to turn ugly over the course of two years? Damn, you act like it's been ten."

We both giggled at that one.

"Well, you know how some women like to make drastic changes to themselves overnight. It's hard keeping up with you women."

There was that phrase: *you women.* I guess that would explain why he never got a relationship out of me.

I said, "Yeah, well, I'm not like all the others. I know what I like, and it doesn't require all that makeover and plastic surgery stuff for me to look good or get a man, you feel me?"

"I hear you, Alex. I always admired your attitude. It's just too fierce for me."

"Ha, which is why so many can't handle me!" I said with a laugh.

"Yeah, you're right. Hey, I don't know if you've been keeping up with me on Facebook or not, but you know I got married just last year," he said.

Oh-em-gee. Is he kidding?

"Really?! That's so exciting, Leon! And truth is, no, I have not been keeping up with anyone lately on social networks. It's too much of a distraction. But I'm excited for you! Congratulations!"

"Thank you, thank you," he said. "My wife Melissa is pregnant with our second child."

I was really excited for him. I did not expect him to ever get married and start a family.

"Aw, that's so sweet. I guess I need to do a better job of keeping up with folk."

"As long as you're not stalking them or anything," he said.

We giggled again. He was so corny, but I laughed to make him feel good. Perfect timing for my phone to ring. I was ready to dismiss myself from this untimely gathering.

"Leon, I have to take this call. I'm going to have to excuse myself," I said as I got up from the table.

"Oh, I understand. Hey, I'll hit you up on Facebook. Nice seeing you."

"Thanks again for paying," I said before walking away.

Ha, that was easier than I thought. It was my good friend Tanisha calling me.

"Hey, girl, guess who I just ran into?" I said in a loud whisper.

"WHO?!" Tanisha screamed so loud, I thought she was going to jump out of the phone.

"Leon Daniels, girl. He got away and started a family and everything."

Tanisha burst out laughing and I felt like I missed the joke.

I asked with a straight face, "What's so funny?"

"I'm sorry, Alex. I just remember when Leon was all over you, and you didn't give him the time of day. Now he's married?"

She was more in shock than I was.

"Yep and has two kids. Well, one on the way," I said, as I began walking to my car.

"Lord . . . well, I'll be. I can't be anything but happy for him. How'd you find all of this out?"

"We ran into each other at Starbucks, and he was nice enough to cover my bill, so we sat and chatted for a bit."

"Ah, he paid your bill, huh? Mmhmm."

Tanisha was a trip.

"It wasn't like that, Tan. Chill that crap out."

"I'm just saying. What're you about to do?" she asked.

"I am headed home to shower and then will probably go shopping later. What's up?"

She said, "I need something to do while Cam is out."

It sounded like a girl's day was in the works, nothing unusual for most Saturdays.

I said, "Okay, well, let me get home and shower, then I'll head over to pick you up."

"Alrighty then. I'll see you in a few."

It felt weird running into Leon after all this time. I had heard he dropped out of law school, which would explain why I never saw him again. Although I had introduced him to my friends, my girl Naomi was the only one to have kept in touch with him. If there was a reason for running into him, I had no clue what it was.

I took a sip of my iced coffee, put my car in drive, turned up my radio, and off I went cruising.

CHAPTER 3

~NAOMI~

Open to finding true love, I took that one-night stand. Brought him home, poured us a glass of my Great American red wine, and sat on my couch. Dinner was great, but there was always a catch to these men I brought home. I was just waiting to see what this one was.

"You have a really nice house, Naomi. It is beautiful," said my date for the evening.

"Why thank you, Kenneth. We haven't even gotten upstairs yet though."

He looked into my eyes.

"What is it?" I asked.

"I'm just admiring your beauty. You have this glow to you. I like it."

I smiled lightly. But I couldn't help but think that he was just buttering me up, saying things a woman wanted to hear. I was so used to it that I had become tired of it.

"Here, put your feet up here," he ordered, as he positioned his lap ready for my size seven feet.

Oh my. A massage? Now, this I am not used to.

"Kenneth, tell me more about you. I'm curious to know."

I was a sucker for story time.

"Well, I gave you all the basics over dinner. What else do you want to know?" he asked.

There had to be more. "Hmm, tell me your favorite childhood memory or how you got into your career or something!"

I could already see he was trying to hold back. I didn't like that.

Kenneth went on to say, "Four years after graduating from college, I worked as a temp for about seven months, then moved up to junior accountant, then finally to executive accountant. I went back to school and got my master's and started working with another company."

For some reason, I was interested in him, but it was too soon to know. Maybe it was the wine. Part of me wanted to cut the small talk and just hop into my bed. But I didn't want to seem like no hoe, so I just chilled.

Intrigued, I replied, "Ah, so you are good with numbers."

"Yes, I am. What got you into the medical field?"

"Well, as a little girl, my mom was sick. She had diabetes as well as lung cancer. None of my older siblings wanted to step up and take care of her, so I did. Can you imagine being a nine or ten-year-old giving your mom insulin and sticking her with needles? I mean, any other kid would be afraid or unwilling. But no, not me."

Opening up to people was definitely not my thing. This just so happened to be the first guy who got me to do it.

"That is tough, yet brave. Is she still living?" Kenneth asked.

"Oh, no. She died when I was fifteen. Been on my own ever since."

"Oh Naomi, I am sorry."

"Don't be, that was so ten years ago."

He continued to massage my feet, which felt so damn good, and that just made me keep talking.

"Ever since she died, I knew that I wanted to help people. So, I went to college and studied nursing."

He was so in tune to what I was saying. I think the wine was getting to him too.

"That is so powerful to me." He licked his lips. Once again, he looked into my eyes and this time, he leaned in for a soft kiss. "How about you give me a tour of upstairs now?"

I grinned and took his hand while leading him up my staircase.

"Nice artwork you have on your wall," he says. "I've always been into really abstract paintings, especially in college. Never could draw or anything though."

I'm guessing this was his way of ignoring the awkwardness. When we entered my bedroom, he immediately started taking his clothes off. I was so used to being the one undressing my partner that I couldn't do anything but stand there.

He gave me a seductive look and said, "You going to stand there all night or you gonna undress?"

Out of all the men I had sex with, this was my first encounter doing things differently. I felt like a rookie standing in my bedroom with my mouth wide open, while Kenneth slowly slipped between my sheets.

"No, I'm coming."

I let out a shy giggle. *Come on, Nai, get yourself together!* Why was this so hard? I slowly removed my short red dress down my chocolate legs, along with my panties and bra, then slid into my covers with his soft and warm yet firm body. For the second time that night, he leaned in and kissed me, but this time passionately. I couldn't help grabbing his cheeks as we dug into each other's lips. He grabbed me, since I weigh only about one hundred and twenty pounds, sat me on top of him, and the inner freak in me just wanted to ride him into the morning.

"Wait a minute," he said, as he grabbed for his pants pocket. Smart move.

I couldn't fault a man for protecting us. That was sexy. He put his little man's coat on and we were back in action. He caressed my plump breasts as they bounced up and down in the air. I was moaning so loud that I was sure my neighbors could hear me, but I didn't care. Meanwhile, I'm sure we were both still a little done in from the wine, but that's when Kenneth flipped me over, and next thing I knew, we were still at it. Good thing the next day was my day off.

Although I wasn't keeping up with the time, it sure felt like we were here longer than we were because Kenneth had exhausted his third condom by now and we took no breaks. But I was a pro and took pride in always lasting longer than the fellas.

"Damn, Naomi, that was some good stuff." Kenneth wiped the beads of sweat from his forehead with the back of his hand.

I let out a sigh. "Yeah, I needed that."

"You want some water or something?"

"Sure, I'll get us some." I motioned to get up and he insisted, "No, I'll get it."

He walked down to my kitchen butt naked, as if he lived here or had been here before. I smiled as I turned over and waited for his return. When he came back, I drank a few sips of water, went to use the bathroom, and hopped back in bed. To my surprise, Kenneth had fallen asleep just that fast. I kissed his cheek as he pulled me in, and we cuddled into the morning.

A few hours later, the sun had come up. When I woke up, Kenneth was not there beside me but his clothes were still on the floor. I grabbed my robe and on my way downstairs, I smelled breakfast.

"Kenneth?"

"Oh hey, I was up so I figured why not cook you something?"

How sweet.

"Aw, Kenneth, that's nice of you. Really."

I sure could get used to a man waking me up to him cooking breakfast in his underwear. But was this too soon?

"Eat up baby," he said as he passed me a plate.

Baby? Hmm. I let it go and just ate my breakfast.

CHAPTER 4

~TANISHA~

I grabbed my purse and headed out the door when I heard the honk of a horn.

My honeymoon had ended a week ago and I was still in relaxation mode. Alex was on her way to pick me up so we could hang and I could enjoy my last weekend off for a while. This was our first time seeing each other since I had gotten married.

As soon as I got in the car, Jill Scott was singing "Golden" and the lyrics couldn't have come at a better time.

"So, Tanisha, simple question: are you happy?" Alex asked, turning down the radio.

"Of course I am, Alex! Like, I'm so in love, it's indescribable. I'm still on cloud nine," I said with a huge grin.

"And how's Cameron?" she asked.

I replied with a sarcastic laugh. "Well, he better be happy. There's nothing more miserable than being in an unhappy marriage."

"Like you would know. Girl, you only been married for what, all of two weeks?"

She was right, but I knew what I was talking about. I couldn't imagine what an unhappy marriage felt like.

"So how's married life so far?" she asked.

That was the question I was prepared to answer from everyone when I got back to work. "For all of two weeks, ahem, it's been . . . well, I mean, how is married life supposed to feel? It's not like we have any kids."

"Well no, but some things ought to feel or be different, right?" Alex asked.

I loved my husband and getting married just solidified that.

"We kiss every day and remind each other that we love one another. I never feel alone with him and he does everything that a wife could ask for."

"Aw, that's sweet, Tan! And being with him just feels like it's right, doesn't it?"

"Yes, Alex!"

I had to admit that the feeling of being a girlfriend was definitely different than being a wife. I felt that I had more duties as a wife to provide to my husband.

"I'm so happy for you and I know I've said this a million times, but I really am, Tanisha. Cameron's a great man."

"Thanks, girl. You're gonna be next."

She said with an almost certain tone, "Ha, yeah right. No time soon."

Alex had been single for as long as I could remember. But I was hoping that would change sooner rather than later. We could use some double dating in our friendship. As we pulled up to the mall, my phone rang. We must've talked my husband up.

"Hey babe, what's going on?"

"I just wanted to call my wife and tell her I was thinking about her."

"Babe, you're too much. Alex and I are at Linfield Mall about to browse through a couple stores."

"Okay, well, I'm going to cook dinner tonight. You want anything in particular?"

Having a man who could cook was a definite bonus since food was the way to my heart.

"No. Anything you whip up is fine with me."

"All right. I'll be home soon. I'm wrapping up this last little bit of paperwork. Talk to you soon."

"Okay, later, babe."

Alex chimed in, "You guys are so sweet. You two give me hope."

I burst out laughing as we walked into the mall. It wasn't that what she said was funny, but I honestly didn't take her seriously because she had been single for so long and was used to it.

"Alex, have you truly gotten over your ex?"

"Girl, yes, that was so three years ago."

"Are you into dating anyone else?"

"Hmm, maybe eventually one day. But right now, I'm all about stacking my coins and taking a vacation from this town. It's not fair you and Cam are the only ones who get to take a break from reality."

She had a point.

That was one of the traits I admired about my friend Alex: she was driven. She never seemed to get distracted or off her game. She was focused on what was important to her in her life at that moment, and if it was her career, then good-bye to relationships for right now.

I replied, "I feel you. And speaking of vacation, I've got two weeks until I go on another one."

"Huh? Where you going now, miss?!" Alex asked like a concerned mama.

"My job has us going to this conference in San Diego for a week. Didn't I tell you about it?"

"No, you did not. Is Cam going too?"

"No, just me, myself, and I. But he'll be all right."

"I'm surprised he didn't try and sneak away with you."

"Well, he has an event to go to during that week and he said his friend wouldn't allow him to miss it."

I was staring down a pair of heels in the store window, even though I had just bought a pair two days before. Shopping was my happy place.

"Ooh, I have an event to go to in a few weeks myself," Alex recalled. " Let me get in here and buy myself something to wear so I can look hot for all the single men."

"Just maybe you'll meet a guy at the event," I said as we entered the store.

"Better yet, maybe he'll meet me," she responded with a flirty look. "But whatever the case, I'm just looking for a good time!"

"High five to that!"

CHAPTER 5

~ALEXANDRA~

"BLACK GIRL POWER! BLACK GIRL MAGIC!"

I was awakened by screaming on my television coming from African American women of all sizes, shades, and hair textures. They graced my screen as a commercial for natural hair shampoo and conditioner came on.

"READ THE PRINTED INK AND KNOCK OUT THAT KINK!"

Wow. When had television commercials become so modernized?

Being a natural sista myself, I had to admit this commercial definitely caught my attention.

The phone rang. I usually didn't answer unknown numbers, but it was a local area code, so I picked it up.

"Alexandra Moore," I said in my office voice.

"No need to be formal, Alex, it's Leon."

"Leon? How'd you get my number?"

"Oh, you can thank Naomi for that."

What in the world was that girl thinking giving this guy my number? If I wanted it, I would have gotten it when I ran into him at the coffee shop a few days ago.

"Yeah, you're right. I will surely be thanking her for that. What can I do for you?"

"Well, first off I apologize if I disturbed you."

"No, you didn't. I dozed off and actually just woke up."

"Oh, okay then. Well, ever since we ran into each other, I have to admit. You have been on my mind."

Uh, where is his wife? "Really? Why is that?"

"Hmm, you know, I can't say. I'm not trying to come off as a creep, Alex. I just wanted to be straight up, you know."

For someone who did not want to come off as a creep, he sure wasn't doing a good job at it.

"I don't know what to say, Leon. And out of all due respect for your wife, I'm not sure this is appropriate."

"Oh trust me, Alex, it's not like she's sitting right beside me. She's actually over one of her girlfriend's house."

And that makes it right?

"Okay, Leon, but I still don't understand why you feel the need to share this."

"It's okay. I wouldn't expect you to understand. Look, I know the past is the past and should remain that way. But when we went our separate ways, it's like all these old feelings started coming back. I got your number from Naomi because I wanted to tell you and I remembered you aren't on social media. Oh, and it would have been tacky to tell Naomi to tell you."

This phone call was leaving me speechless. It wasn't that the feeling was mutual. Nor was it that I was in awe. I was honestly creeped out at this random act of his.

"Wow. You know, I commend you for laying it all out on the table, Leon. Not that this is perfect timing either or anything, but I appreciate you being honest. But I will admit that there are currently no shared feelings amongst us. I'm open to remaining friends with you, of course. But can we just move on and pretend that what just happened did not happen?"

I didn't want to come off as mean. But I needed Leon to understand.

He'd had a crush on me since law school, but I could never give him the attention he wanted simply because my feelings never extended that far for him. He had always been a nice guy, but had a reputation as, well, a loser. That's not to say that Leon was unattractive; he just wasn't *my* type.

Almost in a sour tone, he said, "Totally, that's fine."

"Anything else you care to share before I go?"

"Well, not really. And I'm sorry again if my news was disturbing to you. I really understand."

"Thank you, Leon. I'm going to go and cook me some dinner now. Chat some other time?"

"Of course. See ya."

What in heaven's sake was that about?

I couldn't help but to bust out laughing. I decided to call Naomi right away to burst her bubble—I had no clue what she was trying to accomplish with that move.

Bummer. Straight to voicemail.

She must've been tied up with yet another man.

I didn't want to call Tanisha because she gave me so much hell when I told her about Leon the first time.

I decided to get up and cook myself something to eat while I blasted Pandora.

CHAPTER 6

~NAOMI~

As I sat at the restaurant with this guy, all I could do was think about Kenneth and our experience a few weeks ago. This new guy was being such a pain already.

"You ordered the Mexican tortilla soup? Oh man, my mom tried making that one time and I don't know how she did it but she sure did put her foot in it," said my date as the server delivered my soup to our table.

I delivered a soft and sarcastic giggle.

Between all the clichés and mom references, I was getting fed up. And we were only on our appetizer!

I never understood why I had a hard time with men. A beautiful and sophisticated young lady I was, yet I attracted men who appeared handsome on the outside and terrible on the inside.

"So, can you cook?" he asked.

I responded in a seductive way as I slurped my first bite. "Of course I can. Can you? I love a man who can feed me."

"Well, I can put down a little some-some. My mom taught me when I became a teen."

"Ha, it doesn't surprise me. I'm sure she taught you a lot."

Oops, I didn't mean to be snarky.

"Yes, she did. My dad walked out on me and my brother, so she raised us the best she knew how."

"And there's nothing wrong with that," I assured.

I gave him a weak smile. It was hard not to fault the guy for talking about his mom so much when that was all he knew. And as much as I wanted to end this date already, I couldn't. I would have felt bad.

"So, tell me about yourself, Naomi. Why are you single, if I may ask?"

"I haven't found the perfect match."

"Hmm, is there a specific reason for that or . . . ?"

"Yes, there is. I'm a very picky woman."

"Hard to please, huh?" he asked.

"No, I just know what I like."

I didn't like his attitude. But I was trying to remain calm. It was time to change the subject and get to what I really wanted to know.

I blurted out, "You have any kids?"

"No, not me. But I do have a niece. The most spoiled little girl ever."

"Ha, ha, tell me about it. Everybody used to call me spoiled growing up but I didn't want to accept that label."

As a kid, I always thought I fitted in. Boy, was I wrong. I had it so good that it was the complete opposite: I didn't fit in. While many of my peers had two-parent homes and were not being spoiled on the daily, all my single mom knew how to do was spoil her children. She made sure that we had everything we needed and so much more.

Mark went on. "I can imagine. But there's nothing wrong with spoiling the ones you love, right?"

"Nope, nothing wrong at all," I concurred.

Finally our dinner plates arrived at our table. Your girl was sure enough starving.

"Ah, I see you got the full plate over there."

This was the second time he was all up in my plate.

"Well, you know, a girl has to eat. I see you got the healthy salad going on."

"Yes, ma'am. I have to eat healthy and exercise at least three times a week. Not that you would notice it now, but I used to weigh three hundred pounds."

I almost choked on my bite before my eyes widened.

"Are you kidding? I'm sorry for my reaction."

"Don't be. But no, I'm serious as a heart attack."

That was not the best cliché for him to use in this moment.

Intrigued, I asked, "How did you get rid of the weight?"

"Surgery and change of eating habits."

"Way to go, Mark! What an accomplishment!" I threw my hands in the air like an excited adolescent.

"Thank you. And since I feel that I can be honest with you, you're the first woman I've been on a date with since getting my weight down."

Oh my. See, now I sort of felt like he was pulling the sympathy card or wanted some brownie points. But perhaps this date was a boost of confidence for him since losing the weight.

"Oh Mark, why is that? Never mind, what a stupid question to ask."

"No, no. I had my surgery a year ago last month. I was still trying to recover after the surgery but was also nervous about how women would view me after disclosing that kind of information. But no, don't feel sorry for me or anything. I'm good."

Of course he didn't want me to feel bad for him. His face was handsome, so I didn't feel bad about what he looked like now. His confidence was earning him some cool points and he was still hot to me.

"That's amazing Mark. You know, I wasn't always the confident woman I am today. I had flaws—acne, braces, all that good stuff. Sometimes I would get picked on and teased."

"And how did you overcome that, Naomi?" he asked, looking into my eyes.

I quickly answered before devouring my next bite.

"I went off to college and met some girls who had me join a women's group. They taught you things like building your self-esteem and being independent and loving the person you are. Let them tell it, I was a hot ass mess. But they helped me turn things around for myself."

Mark replied, "That's excellent. My mom used to teach a class at the community center in my old neighborhood for teenage girls who were struggling with their image and such. I thought it was brilliant. She had so many mentees that would come over the house and do 'girl stuff.'"

"Ha, ha, girl stuff? Which includes?"

Having to illustrate with his hands, he replied, "You know what females do: hair, nails, spa crap, and things. You know what I'm referring to."

"Well, isn't that sweet of her? I used to dream of doing something like that. Living in this neighborhood, I see so many teen girls who look like they could use the help."

"You should," he said, delivering a sure look.

Now he was gonna encourage me to pursue my dreams.

"Yeah, well, that's a lot of work and I have to brainstorm more about it," I said passively.

"Do what you gotta do, Naomi. If it helps any, I think you'd be perfect for the job."

So sweet of this stranger to have more faith in me than I did myself. I couldn't believe dinner was turning around for the better.

"You want another round of drinks? My treat?" I asked.

"I'll take another round but let me be a gentleman and treat you, my dear. Server, we'll have another round."

I decided to cut Mama's Boy some slack, at least for tonight. And only because I loved the idea of drinking on someone else's dime.

I wondered where things would go from here. But whatever happened, I had no intentions of bringing him home . . .

Chapter 7

~Tanisha~

"Babe, I'm going to miss you. If only you could come with me." I gave Cameron the sad puppy dog face.

Two weeks had rolled by that quick, and it was Sunday evening, time for one of my occasional work trips. Cameron was dropping me off at the airport right after church.

"Aw, baby, you know I would be getting on this plane with you if I didn't have to go to Mike's benefit dinner party. He's been talking about it for months now," he said.

"Yeah, I know. I'm just being a big baby. Besides, this trip is strictly business. With all that I'll have going on, I probably won't have time for anything fun."

"Just as long as you make time to call me," said Cameron, as he bit his bottom lip.

I smiled. "Oh of course, bae! What kind of wife would I be if I didn't make time for my husband?"

A damn terrible one, I answered in my head.

"Well, you have a safe trip, my love. Make sure you hit me up when you land and are settled."

"I love you, Cam."

We kissed for a few seconds before letting go.

"I love you more, Tan."

It's not that I wasn't used to going away on business trips. This was my first trip away from Cameron since being married, so of course I felt some type of way. I wasn't worried about him. I just missed him already.

As I headed for the gate to where my plane would board, I got a call from Naomi.

"Hey girl, what's up?"

"Hey, Tan. You haven't left for your trip yet?"

"I'm actually about to board my plane now."

"Oh, my bad. I guess I will have to spill the tea to you tonight when you get in."

Oh lord. My girl always had some gossip.

"About your date?" I replied.

"Yeah, the one I went on the other night."

"What happened to Kenneth? You just went on a date with him like two weeks ago."

"Oh we've kept in touch. But ole dude from last night? I told you I don't have time for mama's boys, chile! Girl, he might as well go date his mom instead of trying to impress me, 'cause no one can compete with her!"

Naomi had me cracking up. I looked at her dating life as a game show. She had all these options and yet no one man was good enough. There was always something!

"You got a good point there. Well, let me call you when I land. Let me hop on this plane."

"All right, girl. I'll say a prayer for ya!"

I was sure Naomi would have a story to tell me when I got back about how many dates she had been on since I'd been gone.

While I was in line, I noticed a woman with her child who it seemed she could not control. She was yelling at him to calm down and to stop throwing a fit about getting on the plane. It was clear that he was scared but she did not know how to calm him down.

That's when I remembered the sermon that Pastor had given that morning about how we wrestle and fight with God when it comes to doing things we are afraid of. He told us to step out of our comfort zones and trust that He will carry us through our situation.

I wanted to calmly talk to the little boy, but instead I handed the attendant my pass and entered the jet bridge onto my plane. I threw my headphones in and thought, *San Diego, here I come!*

CHAPTER 8

~ALEXANDRA~

My outfit was spread across my bed, and I jumped into the shower. I was attending a friend's benefit dinner party for his most recent success with his company. I didn't want to go alone, but Tanisha was out of town and Naomi was going on one of her blind dates again. But it didn't matter because I was still single Alexandra and I liked it that way. Besides, I was hoping there would be some cute bachelors out to party tonight.

When I hopped out of the shower, I decided to call my mom. I was the kind of person who cringed when people said that they were best friends with their mom. However, when I got older, my mom became like one of my girlfriends and was often my go-to for a lot of hard decisions I had to make.

"Hey, Ma, how's it going?"

She answered in a jolly tone. "Oh, everything is going just fine. How are things on your end?"

"It's all good over here. I just called to check in on you guys. How is everyone else?"

"Well, Junior is getting his grades up and Ryan is being fast and has another boyfriend."

"Another? What in the world?"

My younger siblings were a mess. I was the oldest of three. My youngest brother was a senior in high school and for so long he struggled to keep his grades consistent. My little sister had just turned twenty-one a few months ago. She was into the carefree, partying lifestyle. My only fear was that she might fall into the trap of what Naomi was doing, and I couldn't have that, which was why I tried so hard to be an example for them both.

"Well, I don't have time right now, but tell her I'll be talking to her real soon about this friend of hers. I'm on my way to a dinner party."

"Oh, that sounds nice. Who's it for?" My mom was so nosy.

"A guy I went to college with. He's been very successful since we graduated and we remained friends, so I figured I'd support him. Oh, and I love to dress up and look nice," I replied as I stood in front of my full-length mirror, admiring my figure.

"Oh my, well, don't let me hold you. Have fun tonight, baby. And don't forget to bring home your future husband. I'll talk to you later."

"Ma!"

She quickly hung up the phone before I could get another word out.

My family lived about an hour away. After I graduated from high school, I moved out and started life on my own. I loved being independent and not having anybody to answer to. I guess you could say I liked my space. But even though I moved away from home, I never once gave up on my brother and sister. I'd always have their backs until the day they died.

CHAPTER 9

~NAOMI~

A few weeks had passed, and I had been on four different dates. Not one of these eligible bachelors passed my eligibility requirements. I was upset, but I was not complaining about all the free wining and dining I was receiving! But shoot, a girl had needs to be taken care of! Out of all the guys I had seen, only one stood out to me: Kenneth. Maybe because he was the only guy who woke up and fixed my greedy ass breakfast. And our conversations were always on point.

It was Friday night and for once, I wasn't out with a man. It was just me and my wine. I knew it had to be the wine that got me thinking about Kenneth. As soon as the doorbell rang, my thoughts went right out the window. I had forgotten that my friend Leon was coming over to help me fix my laptop.

Scuffling over in my bedroom slippers, I managed to open the door.

"Leon, come on in. You'll have to excuse me, I forgot you were coming over."

"Oh my, I just got off the phone with you like an hour ago," he said.

"Yeah, it must be this wine." I held up the bottle.

"Whoa, Nai, why you drinking alone?" he asked.

"I just have a lot going on these days. But I'll be all right. Here, take a look at my laptop."

I grabbed my laptop from the kitchen counter and handed it to him. Leon was a beast with technology, and I just happened to be as dumb as a doorknob in that area, which was why I kept his number on standby.

"So how's Alexandra? Have you talked to her recently?" he asked.

Here we go. I knew my friend would come up in conversation sooner or later. And I really didn't want to talk to him about Alex because I knew she wasn't too fond of him.

I sighed. "She's fine."

"Yes, she is," he responded.

I hit him with the flirty schoolgirl tap on the shoulder.

"Oh stop it, you know that. Give it up already, Leon. She doesn't like you that way. I mean, how many years has it been?"

In a "keep-it-cool" kind of way, he said, "She doesn't have to. I can admire her beauty from a distance."

He reminded me of an annoying young boy who still had the high school crush thing going on—yet he had a wife and kids at home.

"You're a trip. Besides, you lost your chance a long time ago. Now, what's going on with my computer?" I asked, steering the conversation away from Alex.

"Well, it seems you have a virus," he said.

"Oh my gosh. Well, do I need protection or something? I never do pay for those protection service things."

Leon replied, "Luckily it's a mild virus, and I just have to put in a few codes to kill it. Don't worry. I got you."

Whew. He saved my life with that response.

"Thanks so much, Leon. I really appreciate you doing this. Let me pour you a glass to repay you." I knew he wouldn't accept any money.

"Sure," he accepted carelessly.

By now, I'd had at least three full glasses, so I was already feeling good—so good that my clumsy self accidentally spilled a bit of wine on him when I brought him his glass.

As I reached for the stack of leftover fast-food napkins sitting on my counter, I yelled, "Oh Leon, I'm so sorry! Oh no! Let me wipe that off you!"

"It's all right, Naomi, you're good," he said.

Seconds had passed by before I realized I was wiping the inside of his thigh with a napkin. What in the world was I doing? He must've been enjoying it because he sure wasn't saying anything.

Feeling ashamed and somewhat confused, I said, "Uh, I'm sorry, Leon."

"Stop apologizing, Naomi. You're good."

I sat there with my eyes closed, trying to control the whirlwind in my head from the wine. Right when I was about to open my eyes, I felt Leon's soft lips touch mine. I opened my eyes in an attempt to sit up and push him off me.

"Just chill, Nai," he says.

He kissed with such passion. I closed my eyes again, and the image of Leon went out the window. I was now under the impression that I was kissing Kenneth. My hands began to touch his torso and gently move their way down to his belt buckle.

"Nai, you don't have to do this," Leon assured.

I ignored his warning and let my inner freak out from hiding. By now, the wine was in full effect and I was certain that I was with Kenneth right here on my living room couch.

I could hear his moaning, and that was all that was needed to turn my buttons on.

CHAPTER 10

~TANISHA~

I was approaching the last few days of my work trip in San Diego. I was exhausted and ready to come home. *Just one more day,* I kept telling myself. I missed my husband and my girlfriends and had talked to Cameron almost every day since being away. Since there was a three-hour difference between us, I decided to pick up the phone and talk to him before he went to his dinner.

"Hey, baby!" he exclaimed.

"Hey, Cameron! What you up to? You all ready for tonight?"

"Just headed home from work. I'm ready, baby. I got my suit picked out and everything. I just wish I could be with you right now instead," he replied.

Aw, my man missed me. That felt good to know.

"I know you do, babe, but I'll be home in two days. Whatcha gonna do when you see me?"

"Oh, that will be a surprise. Only I know that, for now."

"You so nasty, babe," I said with a huge grin on my face.

Cameron laughed. "Ha, but you like it."

"Well, make sure you send me a nice pic of you tonight. I wanna see what everybody else is gonna see."

I know I seemed desperate, but I just wanted to catch a glimpse of what everyone at that dinner would be looking at. When Cameron dressed up, he was sharp! Besides, you can't blame a girl for being lonely and missing her man.

He said, "Of course, darling. How you feeling?"

"I'm actually a bit tired, but I wanted to talk to you before it got late on your end. I just came from a meeting with the executives. I'm free for the rest of the night, but I'm going to chill for now and take a nap."

"Okay, baby. You get some beauty sleep. I'll FaceTime you in the morning when I get up. I love you!"

"I love you more, Cam."

I really was exhausted from meeting with the bigwigs of my company earlier, so it was time to get some much-needed rest. I had one more day left to enjoy my mini vacation, but all I could think of was relaxation. I turned on the radio to some smooth jazz, and before I knew it, I was out like a lightbulb.

CHAPTER 11

~ALEXANDRA~

I arrived at the dinner party in my gorgeous red knee-length dress and silver pumps. As I stepped out of the Lyft, which I caught because I had planned to get my drink on, I noticed a familiar face across the lot. My ride pulled off and the male figure appeared closer.

I yelled out, "Cameron?!"

"Alex? Hey, lady!"

What was my best friend's husband doing here?

We went in for a hug.

I asked, "What are you doing here? I mean, it's nice to see you and all!"

"Ha, well, same here. You look beautiful tonight. Yeah, Mike and I worked together until he left our company to start his own. How do you know him?"

"Oh well, that makes perfect sense! We went to college together."

I had to admit that I was slightly excited to have another familiar face in the building. But I truly did not expect to run into anyone I knew.

"Oh, that's what's up. Hey, do you mind taking my picture so I can send it to Tan before she flips?" he asked.

"Yeah, sure."

Cameron wore a suave gray suit with a lavender tie. You would've thought he was dressed for Easter. I snapped a couple of pics on his phone so my girl could see what she was missing.

"Thanks, Alex. Let's roll up in here and see what this party is about. That is, if you aren't expecting anyone else."

"Oh no, it's just me," I said.

We entered the hotel, and the hostess directed us to the dining hall where the party was taking place. I could already hear the music pumping as folks were walking around holding onto their glasses. I thought, *This is my kind of party.* I obviously didn't get out much, but when and if I did, I lived for upscale yet chill environments. If only I had a fine piece of eye candy to accompany me.

As soon as we stepped foot into the dining hall, Mike, the honoree of the night, yelled out, "Well, look who it is! You two know each other?! Don't tell me y'all are together!"

We both quickly butted in.

"OH NO! Alexandra is my wife's best friend," shouted Cameron.

I chimed in, "Yeah, I didn't know you worked with Cameron."

"Oh yeah, Cam is my man!" said Mike.

Of course they had to do the bro handshake.

Feeling left out, I said, "Can a sista get some love too?"

"Of course, Alex."

When Mike hugged me, he smelled so nice. I admired men who took time to match their scent with their appearance. I had to give Mike credit. He was a handsome brown-skinned hunk, but I never had eyes for him. I was surprised he was still single. But that didn't mean the women weren't preying on him.

"Feel free to mingle and check out the open bar. We should be getting started very soon. Thanks for coming tonight, guys," said Mike.

"For sure, Mike! Thanks for the invite," I said with a smile.

"Yeah, man, no problem," followed Cameron.

It was time to get my night started. I insisted on getting a drink because I hadn't had one in a few weeks, and as always, work was stressful.

Walking away, I said, "I'm going to the bar, Cameron."

"Right behind you! Especially after the day I had today—whew!"

It looked like Cameron would be my drinking partner for the night.

CHAPTER 12

~NAOMI~

The clock read 12:25 a.m. I woke up on my couch with the wine bottle on the floor. My head was pounding and my living room was dark. What in the world? I checked my phone and saw a text message from Leon.

"YOUR COMPUTER IS FIXED. THANKS FOR THE WINE."

I jumped up and made sure my door was locked. Check.

I checked all my rooms to make sure I was home alone. Check.

I looked at my phone again and reread his text message. Okay, so I remembered Leon coming over to fix my laptop, but that was all. Did we have sex?

I scratched my head and dialed Alex. No shock she didn't answer.

I wanted to call Leon but I knew he was married and I was not about to display myself as "the side chick" because I was not. I didn't have any relations with this man other than a friendship.

I got up, went to the bathroom, and popped a Tylenol in my mouth. I could've just slept this headache off, but I was adamant about finding out what had just happened a few hours ago. *Damn it.* I hated when I got so buzzed and couldn't remember a thing.

"Naomi, what in the world did you do?" I questioned myself.

I plopped down on the couch and threw the covers over my head and attempted to return to sleep. Whatever happened, I would just have to figure it out in the morning . . .

Chapter 13

~Tanisha~

"Aw, look at my baby!"

Cameron had just sent me a picture of himself looking as smooth as they come. I thanked God every day for sending me my Boaz.

I texted him back, "THAT'S MY BABY!"

Here he was out enjoying a night without me and I was sitting miles away in a hotel all alone. But I was getting work done on my laptop and relaxing when I could. Besides, I wasn't feeling very well.

Cam sending me that picture made me think of our future. How it would be if we had children, growing old together . . . it was all part of a dream, but I hoped it would soon become reality.

It was late, but I picked up my devotional book to spend some time with God. The scripture led me to First Timothy, the second chapter.

"A woman should learn in quietness and full submission."

Hmm. This chapter spoke on how a woman should present herself and not assume authority over men. I had no issues with this, but it spoke to my spirit.

After reading, I got down on my knees to pray. I thanked God for the blessings He allowed me to receive and asked Him to continue to use me as He pleased. I was becoming strong in my walk with Christ and strived to live for him more and more each day. I was hoping that Cam was continuing in his daily devotion alone since I wasn't with him.

After prayer, I got into bed, hoping that I would feel better in the morning.

CHAPTER 14

~ALEXANDRA~

The party was over and my blurred eyes read 12:45 a.m. on my phone. I could not believe I had been at this party for four hours! Guys were staggering out the door and women had heels in their hands. Eventually Cameron and I had split up at some point in the night. But it was time to head home. I left the dining hall and found him in the hallway laughing hysterically with some of his buddies.

I walked up to him and said, "Cameron, I'm headed home."

Why was I giggling? Oh yeah, I was drunk, myself.

"I'll hit y'all up," he said to his buddies. "Oh, what'd you say, Alex?"

I whispered, "I was just telling you I'm gone," and headed for the exit.

"You can't drive, girl. You drunk as hell," he slurred, along with a chuckle.

"How would you know? You drunk yourself!"

We couldn't help but laugh because we were both wasted. I was pretty sure I had more than the bartender should have given me.

"Besides," I said, "I caught a Lyft here, so I didn't drive. You gonna make it home okay?"

"You didn't drive? Okay. You can ride with me." Cameron flashed the keys to his Buick Regal.

"You don't have to do that. I'll send for a Lyft right now." I pulled my phone out of my purse.

I was so modest that when people wanted to be nice to me, I did not want to accept it. I never wanted to impose on anyone, and that included those close to me.

He said smoothly, "Alex, you my girl. And it's no problem."

"Well, okay."

We made it outside to the car. I had to walk barefoot because my feet were hurting in my pumps. Before I realized it, Cameron was leaning over in the bushes, releasing the festivities of the night from his soul.

"Cam, you all right?"

He mumbled something. I staggered over to him and grabbed his keys. There was no way I was going to let him drive. Granted, I was drunk myself but he couldn't drive and throw up at the same time.

"Come on, get in. I'm driving us."

***

We arrived at my place after 1:30 a.m. I parked in my driveway because only my car was in it. I figured if he needed a minute to get himself together, he could just chill at my place.

"Cameron, you wanna come in and get yourself some water?"

There was that mumble again. Oh lord, was I going to have to help him and myself into this house?

I went and opened the door to my house so I could just walk him right in. Although I was drunk, there was that instinct to make sure that others around me were good. I came back to grab Cameron, who was dead weight. I was sure this guy weighed at least 180 or so compared to my 140. But being drunk made it all worse.

I finally got him into my house.

"Where am I?" he mumbled as he finally opened his eyes.

Out of breath, I replied, "You're at my place. Here, just rest on the couch for a while."

I gently shoved him onto the couch, and he grabbed me so that I ended up falling on top of him.

"Cameron, let go! What're you doing?"

"Mmm. You smell good. What are you wearing?" he asked, sniffing my neck and attempting to plant kisses on me at the same time.

"Cameron, I am Alex. Not Tanisha. Get off me," I responded firmly. He released me and I slid my way to the kitchen and grabbed us both a bottle of water and some crackers for Cameron. I return and say, "Here, drink this. And if you have to throw up again, please let me know."

After guzzling half of his water, he said, "Come here."

What? This guy is tripping. I could barely keep my eyes open and at this point I was dizzy from the effort it took to get him on my couch.

"Cameron, go to sleep. It's two a.m."

"Come, sit here." He patted his lap as if he was Santa. And I sure as hell didn't want no gifts from him. "You sit over there," he blurted out.

Huh? He wasn't making sense. I flicked on the television and sat on the opposite side of the couch for a few seconds more before I had the thought to retreat to my bedroom.

Next thing I knew, Cameron had jumped on me and began kissing me. All I could feel was his hard-on pressing up against my leg. What exactly was happening? I knew but I was too out of it to fully comprehend.

"Cam . . . "

"Shhhh," he whispered, placing his finger over my lips.

All of a sudden, my intoxicated mind overtook my conscious thoughts. It was like part of me was super drunk but the other part was sober—like the angel and the devil present on each shoulder.

He took off his shirt. As he unzipped his pants, I found my body ready to receive him. He lifted up my dress and began kissing my stomach.

"Cameron, get off—"

"Stop it," he demanded.

The angel on my shoulder told me to get up and push him off. But his weight was so heavy. The devil told me this was someone else and to just lie there and endure it because I was drunk and horny.

By this time, his pants were down to his ankles and my dress was raised to my stomach. He kissed me, I kissed back. When he got down to my neck, I couldn't help but moan. That's when all hell broke loose.

CHAPTER 15

~NAOMI~

It was Saturday morning and for the life of me, I could not figure out what happened between Leon and me the previous night. Alex still hadn't returned my calls, and I knew Tanisha was either asleep or busy with work. I couldn't help but wonder what Alex would think when I told her I may have slept with the guy who liked her but whom she had no interest in. She would probably shame me.

I texted Leon and asked him to meet me at the coffee shop on Twenty-First Street. To my surprise, he agreed. As I sat and waited for his arrival, the server walked up to me.

"Is there anything I can get you? Would you care for a menu?"

"No thank you, I'm just waiting on someone. Quick business, then I have to run," I replied.

With a smile, she said, "Okay, no problem."

She walked away and there stood Leon.

"Oh shoot, Leon, don't creep up like that."

"Ha, I'm sorry, Naomi. You haven't ordered anything?" He sat down.

Giving direct eye contact, I said, "No, I'm kind of in a rush. I just wanted to chat with you quickly about last night."

"What about it?" he responded passively.

Now he was going to act like he had a loss of memory.

"Were you drunk?" I asked him.

"Truthfully, no. But you were."

"I know that. But what happened?"

"Uh, let's just say I should've paid money for the service I received," he said, grabbing a menu from the table to browse.

I wasn't following him. I wished he would be straight up and spit it out.

"What services, Leon? I'm not a stripper, so did I dance for you or something?"

"Okay, I'll just say it. You got down on your knees and rocked the mic."

I was about ready to flip because one, I didn't like these hidden messages he was giving. And two, did he just say I put my mouth on him?

"Leon, you—"

"You gave me head," he blurted out.

I burst out laughing, sure he was joking. "You're kidding, right?"

"No. You wanted the truth; there you have it," he said with a straight face.

"No more, no less?"

"That was it. I mean, you did try to go the extra mile and actually have sex with me, but I put a stop to it."

This mother flipper. "Hmm, okay. So you weren't drunk, yet you didn't stop me from going down on you?"

"I know it sounds bad, but you can't just point the finger over here. I don't control you, Naomi."

He had his nerve.

"Leon, I will apologize for being drunk. But I'm disturbed that you did not prevent what happened from happening."

"Okay. Naomi, look, I will apologize as well for allowing that to take place. I shouldn't have taken advantage of you in your weak moment. But I'm a man. And I know that doesn't mean anything to you . . . " He motioned for the server to return to our table.

What did he mean that didn't mean anything to me? Was he implying that because he was a man, I should accept his actions?

"Uh, excuse me?" I said defensively.

"What I'm trying to say is I, myself, was not drunk, but I was clearly caught in a weak moment. That doesn't make what happened right though."

How pathetic it was for him to sit there and deny responsibility for his selfish and "I'm just a man" behavior. I wanted to reach across the table and slap him but the server walked over right in time. I went on as if she wasn't standing there.

"Leon, you've got a lot of nerve trying to blame me. Now, I shouldn't have been sloppy and messy and exhibiting hoe-like behavior. But honestly, being drunk is no excuse either. I didn't think it was you who I was entertaining. In my head, it was someone else."

The server, now standing there in full awkwardness, looked at Leon.

"I'm sorry, ma'am," he apologized. "May I get a large coffee, black?"

"Sure. Be right back."

Leon continued, "That's understandable. And respectfully, I never have looked at you in that kind of way."

He might not have viewed me in that way, but he couldn't sit there and act like I was not an attractive sista. I just wanted to squash this incident and put it behind us as if it never happened. But there was one more thing I wanted to clear up.

"I guess that's nice to know. But Leon, can I just make an observation?"

"Yeah, sure."

"You are married, correct?"

"Well, legally yes."

Here we go. What was he hinting at now?

I asked, "What do you mean 'legally' yes?"

He sighed as if about to make a confession.

"Melissa and I are married, yes. But it's difficult."

"How is it difficult and y'all have only been married for almost a year and a half?"

He was not making sense.

"I love her, but I'm not sure we should be together. Ever since we got married, things have made a drastic turn. She's six months' pregnant, so she has her moods, nothing I do is enough, and there's a lot of bickering and tension in our relationship."

I felt like I was playing the shrink. "Did you not see any signs before marriage?"

"No, I didn't. Melissa can be the sweetest woman when she wants to. She'd do anything for our child. But I'm not sure she'd do *anything* for me."

Wow. He dropped a bombshell.

Feeling my heart softening, I said, "Wow Leon, I had no idea you were going through this."

"Yeah, I try to paint a smile on and live life the best I can. But oftentimes I find myself at the bar getting wasted all while trying to clear my head on what to do," he said.

I didn't want to turn all Christian on him, but something nudged at me to do so. "Have you talked to God about it?"

"Now, Naomi, you know I'm not into church and religion."

"Well, maybe you should give it a try. Just this once. For the sake of not losing the best thing that could ever happen to you and so that things like last night won't happen to other people. I mean, you can't cheat on your wife, Leon. That's foul."

I made myself sound like a victim but I was just as guilty if not more.

"You know, I'll give it a try. But man, something has to be done. I'm about to lose it," he said as the server returned with his coffee in hand.

"I have faith in your marriage. Just don't give up yet. But I'm going to run now. I'll check you later." I got up from the table. "Oh, and thanks again for my computer."

"No problem. Naomi. Thanks for being a listening ear."

With a light smile, I said, "No problem."

Despite what happened last night, I had a good heart. I loved to help people with their problems knowing I had my own to work through. It seemed to be much easier to help others with their issues than to focus on myself. I was moving on from the situation and had already forgiven Leon in my heart. I still wanted to tell my girl Alex, but I had to find her first.

CHAPTER 16

~TANISHA~

It was Saturday, my last day to enjoy my trip. Since it was the weekend and I had finished my duties for my job, I figured I would treat myself to the spa. I woke up feeling better than I did the night before. I had no idea what was bothering me but after drinking some ginger ale, my stomachache went away. It was morning in Detroit, so I hit up Cam to check in. He didn't answer, which was odd.

I thought maybe he was still asleep and had a long night. After I took a shower, I tried calling again.

No answer. I left a voicemail this time.

"Hey baby, it's me. Just called to say good morning and hear your voice. Talk to you soon. Love you."

I didn't want to come off as overly aggressive, but he should have checked in by now and anxiously spilled the events of last night. While deciding on an outfit for the day, I dialed Alex. I knew *she* would answer.

"Hey, you've reached Alexandra. Leave me a message."

I hung up before the beep. I knew she also had an event last night, so maybe she was sleeping in as well.

Where was everybody?

My last resort was to call Naomi. I loved my friend, but I didn't have time to hear her talk about her shenanigans.

"Hello?" she answered.

"Hey Nai."

"What's up, girlfriend?! I feel like I haven't talked to you in forever!"

I replied dryly, "It's only been a week."

"Well, yeah, I know but I didn't want to bother you while you were handling business. You'll be back tomorrow, right?"

"That's the plan. Have you talked to Alex?" I asked, while modeling my possible outfit choices in the mirror.

"Nope. I called the girl a couple times and she has yet to return my call."

Hmm. Seems I'm not the only one.

I said, "I tried calling her as well. I know she had a party last night. Oh well. Maybe she'll call us back soon."

"Maybe. How's Cam?"

"Yeah, I tried calling him too. No answer."

Naomi replied, "That's strange. Where these heifers at?!"

"Girl, you tell me. I'm the one who's miles away. Well anyway, I'm getting ready to head to the spa then brunch. I'll text you in a few."

"Okay, girl," she said and hung up.

Where were these two? Both partied out? Must have been some party for each of them. I just let it go and got dressed to head out into the nice San Diego weather for the last time.

CHAPTER 17

~ALEXANDRA~

I woke up in my bed sweating and half naked, blinking multiple times to make sure that I was in my right mind. Then I remembered.

Cameron.

I put on my robe and ran down the stairs to find Cameron sitting on my couch, half asleep but with the television still on.

I called out, "Cameron."

He raised his head and turned around as if I had startled him.

"Uh, good morning," he said with a raspy voice.

"You're still here. Would you like a cup of coffee? I-I-I'm gonna fix myself some," I said uneasily.

"Yeah, sure."

I didn't want to say much because I wasn't sure how much he remembered about last night.

My kitchen clock read 11:30 a.m. Thank God it was Saturday.

As I was fixing coffee, I tried to replay what happened the previous night. All I could remember was trying to be a good friend and helping my girl's husband, who was super intoxicated. Should we talk about what happened? Or just put this incident behind us and never bring it up again?

Cameron was a very attractive guy, but I never thought of him in a sexual way. And I would never do something like that to my best friend. I was sure there was a handbook of the "Do's and Don'ts" between best friends, and I had violated the rules 110 percent.

I brought Cameron a cup of coffee, which he graciously accepted as if he were a homeless man receiving a meal.

"Well, I'm headed upstairs to shower. Do you need anything else?" I offered.

"No, I'm actually gonna bounce in a second."

"Okay, just let yourself out."

I walked away thinking I'd ignore everything and move on.

"Alex? Can we talk real quick?"

Oh shoot. I guess we have to face the facts sooner or later. It's only right. Reluctantly, I responded, "Uh, yeah. Sure."

I joined him on the couch. He turned the television off as if to say he meant business.

After a brief pause, he said, "Look, about last night. I take full responsibility for what happened. You can't imagine how I feel right now."

"You're right, I can't. But you also can't imagine how I feel. All that's on my mind is my best friend and how I may have just ended our friendship."

"Friendship? What about my marriage?!"

Was he raising his tone at me in my house as if I said something wrong?

"Cameron, we both have to take full responsibility because we are grown and being drunk doesn't give us a pass. I understand how you feel, but I don't think I asked for it to happen. I didn't make the first move."

He looked up and I noticed his eyes were red. I couldn't tell if it was from the lack of sleep or if he had been crying.

He said, "I see why you would say that. I'm so hurt. Like, I really messed up. I don't want you to believe that I had that planned or something. In honesty, I had too much to drink. I can admit that. But that does not mean that my actions were okay and I apologize."

I really did not want what happened to put us in a bad place. But if Tanisha ever found out about this, the both of us might end up dead.

"I don't know, Cameron. I don't know how to move on from this."

His phone lit up and the screen flashed a picture of him and Tanisha. She was calling and my heart dropped. I was hoping he wouldn't answer.

"Dammit. What am I going to do, Alex?"

I actually felt bad for his marriage more than my friendship. We were both on the verge of possibly losing someone who meant so much to us.

"Either we come clean and confess or bury this for dear life," I suggested.

"Which would you do?" he asked.

"Well, because I'm not a liar, I would just come clean to her. I know it would hurt her, but in the end, I would feel better getting it off my chest."

I was being honest.

Cameron got up and grabbed his belongings. "I've got some things to think about. She comes back in town tomorrow."

"Well, you have to decide by then. But it's your choice, not mine," I said.

"Should we confront her together?"

"Umm, I'm not sure. Just give it a couple days."

He walked out the door.

At that moment I was not able to fully process what was going on. I wasn't sure that I could ever look at Cameron the same from now on. But in my heart I forgave him because it was the Christian thing to do. But I had no idea how "Christian" Tanisha would take the news if and when she ever found out.

CHAPTER 18

~NAOMI~

I was at the gym getting an intense workout. I had to keep my shape right for Mr. Right, whoever that would be. My phone rang and lo and behold, the name "Alex" popped up on my screen. It was about time this chick called me back. I pushed the stop button on the treadmill and answered the call.

I answered breathlessly, "Alex?! Where in the . . . world have you . . . been hiding?!"

She screamed at me, "Why are you breathing so hard?! Don't tell me you are in the middle of getting it in and you answering my call!"

"Girl, don't play." I couldn't catch my breath and she had the nerve to make me laugh. "I'm at the gym."

"This late? Who you showing off for, Naomi? Hmm. It must be some sexy fellas in there at night, huh?"

"Girl, bye. I called you like fifteen times between yesterday and today. You must've had a hot date or something." I quickly diverted the attention back to her.

"Yeah, about that. I had some things going on."

"Mmhmm, well, I had a few things on my plate too that I wanted to dish to you. You got time?" She better have after avoiding me all this time.

"Sure, spill."

I didn't know how she would take it. But there was no point in holding back now. I went and found a seat to prepare myself for this curse-out.

"Well Alex, I told you how my laptop was messed up, right?"

"Mmhmm."

"And I called on Leon to come by and fix it for me, right?"

"Mmhmm."

She appeared to be calm, so I kept going. She had no idea where this was heading.

"Well, one thing led to another and I gave him some."

The line grew quiet.

"Some what?" she asked.

"Some sloppy top," I replied.

Alex burst out laughing. Here I was thinking she was going to be upset.

She screamed, "GIRL! I THOUGHT YOU WERE GONNA SAY YOU GAVE HIM SOME COOKIE!"

"And would it still have been funny?!" I asked, sitting there confused by her laughter.

"Girl, no. Either way, I don't care. Did you think I was going to be mad or something?"

"Uh, no. But I thought you were going to curse me out!" I had to laugh myself looking back at it.

"Well, you are twenty-five years old, and anything that makes you happy makes me happy," Alex said.

She had a point.

She added, "Besides, I already know you a fast-ass, so I'm not shocked."

"Don't do me like that," I responded with an eye roll.

"But how did that happen? You like him or something?"

"You are funny. No, I don't like Leon. And I was drunk when he came over."

Still fishing for answers, she asked, "So how do you know what you did?"

"He told me."

"And you believe him?"

I hated how Alex always twisted things to make me think even harder and read between the lines.

"Yeah, why would he lie?"

She yelled, "'Cause he's a man!"

"Yeah, but you know Leon. He's not like that."

Alex grew heated.

"Oh yeah? Well, what about his wife? Does she know about this?!"

She was about to fly off the handle as if she were my mother. There was a reason I gave her the nickname "Mama Alex," and that was because she never judged me for my decisions. She only encouraged me to make sense out of why things happened the way they did.

"Nah, she doesn't," I said. "But I questioned him about that too. He said things between them are rocky."

"And so because of that, he cheats on her?"

"Pretty much."

"Now, Naomi—"

I quickly cut her off. "Calm down. I spoke to him and gave him some advice."

"Oh really? Well, let me give you some advice. And I'm saying this the nicest way possible because you're my girl and I love you," she reasoned.

Uh oh. Now she was sounding like my mother instead of my friend for real.

60

"Okay, Alex."

"I don't care who you mess around with. But be careful who you mess around with. Especially with these married men. Don't make a fool of yourself or get yourself in something that you can't get out of. I don't care if it is Leon," she said.

"Oh Alex, don't trip. I don't touch the married fish. Leon was the first and last. Besides, it's not like this was planned."

"It never is planned, Naomi. Just be careful, okay?"

I had to give her points on this one. She was making sense. And it wasn't like I'd never heard this one before. Moving on, I said, "I know. So, enough about me. Where were you last night? Tanisha said she called you a dozen times."

"Yeah, I saw she called me. But I can't talk about that right now. I'm actually going to read my lesson for church tomorrow. I'll see you then," Alex said.

"Oh, well, okay. I'm going to head home myself. See you tomorrow."

It was almost as if this conversation had hit a nerve or something for Alex. She just went off on me! I knew my friend, and I knew she was hiding something, but I wasn't going to press her. I figured she'd tell me when the time was right.

CHAPTER 19

~TANISHA~

When I saw my baby waiting for me at the terminal, I made a dash like a child running to its father. I missed my husband!

"Hey, baby!" said Cameron as I jumped into his arms.

We kissed for at least a good minute. It felt so good to be back in my husband's arms after a week.

"Cameron, I missed you like crazy! Everything okay?!"

"Yeah, baby. You know I missed you too. Let's get out of here."

He took my hand and grabbed my suitcase. When we arrived home, Cam already had dinner prepared. He also had the nerve to make my favorite: fried chicken! But for most of the car ride home, he was too quiet for comfort. And I could feel that something was wrong.

We sat at the table and talked over dinner.

"So, how have things been around here? I'm shocked to say that I actually missed home."

I had to break the silence and chewing of fried chicken because I couldn't stand a quiet dinner.

"Things have been the same," he responded safely and quickly.

"You never talked to me about the benefit dinner party! How was it?"

"Uh, it was so-so. Not really what I expected."

"How come? It must've been some kind of party. You didn't talk to me almost all weekend."

Crunching on his piece of chicken, he said, "Yeah, I got home pretty late. A lot of drinking and music. You know Alexandra was there."

I stopped chewing for a second.

"Really? What was she doing there?"

"She's mutual friends with Mike," he said.

"Oh, I didn't know. That explains why she talked about having a party the same exact night! I bet she looked nice! I was with her when she picked out her dress!"

Cameron replied, "Uh, yeah. She fit right in with the rest of the women."

"Oh how nice. I haven't talked to her in a few days."

"She was at church today," he said, waving his chicken bone.

I forgot all about it being Sunday. I was just happy to be back home.

"Oh, ooh," I moaned as I rubbed my belly.

Cameron asked, "You okay, baby?"

Suddenly that pain in my abdomen was back again.

"Yeah, I've just been having pains in my belly for the last week. I'm fine. Just get me some ginger ale, will you?"

I had no idea what had been pinching at my stomach for a few weeks now. But I was sure that I would have to soon make a visit to the doctor to see about it.

Cam brought me a can of ginger ale and I threw it back like it was a shot.

"Slow down, baby. It's not going anywhere."

"Yeah, well, I'm finished with dinner. I'm going to lie down. Maybe you'll join me after you clean up the kitchen?" I gave him a wink, hoping he would get the clue.

"Uh, yeah, sure. Go lie down, babe. I got this."

I headed upstairs and changed into my lingerie. Although I was in a bit of pain, I hadn't seen my husband in a week, so of course I was pining for him. I had planned on making my move on him when he joined me in the bedroom. While I waited, I called Alex to let her know I was back in town.

"Hey, you've reached Alexandra. Leave me a message."

I was sure this girl was ignoring me by now. Did I do something to her? Or was she just plain busy? Whatever the case, I had my mind on something else: my man. And I couldn't wait for him to join me.

CHAPTER 20

~ALEXANDRA~

It was Monday morning and back to work. With all the events that took place over the weekend, my mind was not in any position to focus on paperwork.

"Ms. Moore, you have a phone call on line one," my assistant buzzed in.

"Thanks, Taki."

Fearful of who it might be, I answered professionally. "This is Ms. Moore. With whom am I speaking?"

"No need to be formal, it's Tanisha."

I took a big gulp and my heart felt like it was in my stomach.

"Tanisha, hey. I'm sorry."

She said, "It is so hard keeping up with you, girl. I figured the only way to catch up with you is at work. I've been calling your cell all weekend."

As if I didn't know that. I saw those calls. She just didn't know there was a reason for me avoiding them.

"Yeah, about that. I had a tough weekend. I had some paperwork that actually had to be reviewed before this morning, so my hands were tied," I responded with a lie.

"It's cool."

"How was your trip?" I asked her.

"It was nice—equal parts relaxation and work. How was your party?"

Oh shoot. She was inching. I wondered if Cameron had told her that I was in attendance.

With a light chuckle, I said, "Girl, that party was too much. Had a lot to drink of course. Food was good too."

"Oh okay. Cameron told me that you were there as well. You're mutual friends with the guy, right?" Tanisha asked.

"Yeah, small world, huh? I had no idea that Cam's party was my party. But it was nice."

I wondered what else he had told Tanisha. But it couldn't have been too much because she was too jolly. Unless it was the calm before the storm.

She went on to say, "Yeah, he must still be tired from the weekend because I tried to have sex with him last night and he wasn't having it. Do you know how frustrated I was?! Girlllll."

"Oh no. Maybe it was just bad timing. You know every time we want it, they don't. But when they want it, we have to stop everything we're doing."

I felt so bad.

Tanisha replied, "Girl, yes, look at you talking like you got some recently."

"Well, you know, just because I'm not looking for anything long term right now doesn't mean I don't know about the opposite sex."

We both laughed.

"I know that's right. Have you talked to Naomi?" she asked.

"Yeah, I have. Did she tell you she had relations with Leon?"

"Relations? Girl, no. What kind of relations?"

"The kind that involves getting on your knees and speaking into the mic."

We both laughed again. I missed my best friend. But it was the truth that was holding me back from opening up to her and being normal. Any conversation that didn't involve me was the goal.

"Well, I'm sure she was heard, all right. That child is a trip, you hear me!" Tanisha said.

"Loud and clear. Well, I hate to cut you off, Tan, but I have a meeting coming up in a few."

"It's okay. I need to get back to business myself. I'm working from home today so I'm easily distracted."

"Ha, I hear ya. Talk to you soon."

"All right."

I let out a huge sigh of relief when I hung up that phone. *Lord, what do I do now?* I couldn't figure out if I should consult with Cameron once again or just spill the beans on my own terms. I felt like I shouldn't speak on it without him knowing. I could at least give the brotha a warning first. But we had to do something soon because treading lightly like this could not go on too much longer.

CHAPTER 21

~NAOMI~

I had finally gotten Alex to agree to come to lunch with me. I knew she would have to get back to work soon, but I wanted her to let whatever was bothering her out. We were best friends and her secrets would always remain safe with me.

"So, what's up, Alex?" I asked, starting this lunch date off in a sharp tone.

"Huh? What do you mean?"

"Girl, don't 'huh' me. Something is bothering you."

"Naomi, I just came to eat with you on my lunch break. Why the interrogation?"

"Oh, I haven't even begun to interrogate you yet! But seriously, I know you. And I know that you are hiding something."

"Is it that obvious?" she said sarcastically.

"To your best friend of four years, yes."

She took a deep breath. "I slept with Cameron."

I spit my sip of water out.

"YOU WHAT?!"

Before I knew it, the other guests in the restaurant were looking over at our table. Talk about starting a scene.

"I'm sorry, Alex, I didn't mean to yell," I said calmly.

"It's okay."

Little did she know she had just ruined my appetite. I wasn't one to judge because I knew I had some baggage of my own. But this?!

Proceeding with caution, I asked, "One question: how?"

Hesitantly, she answered, "Well, we both attended Mike's party Saturday night. He and I got super drunk and I tried to be a good friend and let him stay at my place and sober up."

"And one thing led to another?"

"Kind of. I had no intentions of ever letting things get that far. It just happened. When I woke up the next morning, I felt so out of place."

Alex was in the most compromising place she could be. There was no doubt in my mind that she was telling the truth about whatever took place between her and Cameron, and that this whole thing was a mistake—I could see her brokenness.

"Wow, Alex. I see we both had our share of drinking this past weekend. So are you going to tell Tan?"

"That's the thing. I've been avoiding her as much as possible. I want to tell her but she will probably never look at me the same."

Probably? We both knew Tanisha and that probably was a definite negative.

"If it's in her heart to forgive you and remain best friends, then she will. But I've got to admit, Alex, that's a huge load you got on you. I wouldn't want to be in your shoes right now," I said reassuringly.

I felt bad for my girl. Lord, why couldn't it have been anybody else?

Alex asked, "If I go to her and explain the truth like I just did to you, do you think she will believe me?"

"Well, maybe not. But if Cameron is there and can account for the truth as well, it might help."

She took a pause.

"I just don't want her to think I'm a liar and that I intentionally slept with her husband."

She had a point. Cameron really was a nice-looking gentleman. That's admitting the truth. But of course he was off limits.

"Like I told Leon, pray on it. What's meant to be between y'all will be," I said as I rubbed her shoulder, trying to be of comfort.

"I just need some time." Alex took a deep breath.

"Of course, take all the time you need. I feel in my spirit that your friendship will be a bit strained, but after some Jesus gets in the middle of it, you two will be fine," I replied with a slight chuckle.

Alex shook her head. "Naomi, you a mess."

"I'ma have to start charging people for my word. Give an offering when you come to the table, ya dig?"

We both laughed and continued with our lunch.

CHAPTER 22

~TANISHA~

By now, I had been back home for a whole week. Between my belly acting crazy and Cameron not wanting to be intimate with me, I was sure that something was not right. I picked up my cell phone and dialed my doctor's office. I loved the joy of working remotely so that I could take care of both personal business and my job work at the same time.

My doctor's receptionist told me the earliest appointment would be on the following Tuesday.

"Next Tuesday? Why do I have to wait a whole week?"

She answered politely, "Dr. Marabi is booked for this week, ma'am. I'm sorry but that's the best I can do."

I wasn't sure if I could wait another week. I had already been suffering for three weeks now.

"Well, put me down for next Tuesday. If I can't hold out until then, I'll just have to go to the ER. Thank you."

I hung up the phone.

I didn't want to worry Cameron or even myself. But I had to go to the doctor and find out what was up because I was sure that this was not just a stomachache. It had been bothering me for almost a month now. To have to wait another whole week was ridiculous. But my pain level wasn't as bad as before, so maybe I could hold out.

Maybe I was stressing out about my husband. He had been acting weird ever since I came back home. His mind seemed to wander off, like he was in another world or deep thought. Right then and there, I broke out into prayer.

"Lord, I'm not sure what's ailing me and causing my body to be in pain. But I know you're a healer and that you can fix whatever this is. I ask that you take control of my body from head to toe. And Lord, whatever is going on with my husband, please let him know that he's not alone and that we are a union. I don't want to feel like I'm losing my husband two and a half months into our relationship. Restore us in Jesus' name."

CHAPTER 23

~ALEXANDRA~

Earlier in the day, I texted Cameron and asked him to call me when he had a free moment. I knew that he would have a break after work before he coached basketball at the community center. That was the only time I figured he wouldn't be around Tanisha. Just as I was packing up to go, my cell phone rang. It was him.

"Hey Cameron," I said dryly.

"Hey, Alex. I got your text. Everything okay?" He sounded worried.

I tried to answer in a normal tone. "Yeah, everything's fine."

Who was I kidding?

"Well, I mean no. Everything isn't fine," I quickly rescinded.

"What's the matter?" he asked as if he didn't know.

I said firmly, "You know what the matter is. We need to handle this."

"Ohhh, that. Okay."

I wasn't sure how he was making out sleeping beside his wife and harboring a secret that could destroy their marriage. But my thoughts kept me up at night and distracted me from functioning normally. I took Naomi's advice and talked to the Lord. I was sure He gave me His answer. "We have to tell her, Cameron. The Lord said so."

"Alex, I hear you. I prayed about it too. But I'm still uncertain."

"About?"

"About coming clean of course. I want to be open and honest. But I also want my wife to remain my wife."

I took a deep breath. "And you think the best way for that to happen would be to keep quiet?"

He sighed.

"No. But you're right. Let's tell her."

Thank God he was in agreement. Did he honestly think this was something so minor that we could give it a pass?

"Okay. When and how?"

"Let's do it tomorrow, Alex. Come over and we'll take things from there."

"Okay. Thanks, Cameron," I said and hung up.

This made no sense. I was plotting behind my girl-friend's back. But Naomi did encourage me to be straight up and I didn't want to be straight up without Cameron knowing my game plan. I grabbed my belongings and headed out of the office.

Chapter 24

~Naomi~

It was Wednesday, my day off, and I was excited to be spending time with Kenneth. We hadn't seen each other since our first date, but we had been texting ever since. It was Kenneth's idea to take me to the aquarium. I loved an adventurous man.

We were watching the sharks swim around the tank. So romantic.

"Take my picture, will you?" I asked, handing him my phone.

"You women always want to take pictures when y'all go out!"

I laughed and said, "You just hating. We like to capture memories!"

I stood next to the gigantic tank full of sharks as he took my picture.

"Take one with me," I said.

"You a trip," Kenneth replied, shaking his head with a mild grin.

I took a selfie of us. This was definitely a moment to remember.

"Naomi, can I ask you something?"

"Sure, what is it?"

"Why are you so gorgeous?"

I gave a flirty laugh. But there was no need to flirt with Kenneth. We were just buddies.

"You have to ask my momma that!"

"Well, give me the number to heaven and I'll call and ask her," he said.

I loved that Kenneth had a sense of humor. He was also smooth with his flirtatious jokes and knew when to deliver them.

My cell phone rang and I wondered who would have the nerve to interrupt my date. It was Tanisha.

"Nai, are you busy?" she asked, breathing heavily.

"Kind of. Why? What's up?" I was getting worried.

"Do you think you can come get me and take me to the ER?"

"Yeah, what's wrong?!"

"I'll tell you when you get here. Just please hurry."

"Okay, I'll be there in twenty minutes." I hung up and started walking and took Kenneth's hand.

"What's wrong, Naomi?" He picked up a swift walking pace alongside me.

"Sorry to cut our date short, but we have to take my girl Tanisha to the hospital," I said.

Understandingly, he replied, "Oh, okay. Let's go."

I wasn't sure why she had asked me to take her and not her husband. But it didn't matter at the time. I had to be there for my friend.

CHAPTER 25

~TANISHA~

Thank God for best friends. I was happy that Naomi was able to bring me to the hospital in the middle of her date. I didn't want to worry Cameron while he was at work, but eventually Naomi called both him and Alex and they were on their way. I tried holding out until my appointment but my body just wasn't having it.

Sitting in my bed in the outpatient room, I said, "Thanks again, Naomi. And you too, Kenneth, I really appreciate this."

"No problem, Tan. I got you. So what did the doctors say?" asked Naomi.

"They took my blood and ran a few tests. Hopefully they can tell me something soon."

"I really hope so. I don't like seeing you like this."

"I'm not worried. God's got me," I said.

At that moment, Alex walked through the door.

"Hey y'all, I got here as soon as I could. What's going on?"

"We're still waiting for the doctor to tell us," I replied.

Alex smiled. "Well, I know God to be a healer, and whatever it is, you will get through it."

Cameron barged in a few seconds behind her. "Baby, you all right?! Why didn't you call me?"

In a calm and reassuring tone, I replied, "Cam, I didn't want you to worry. I'm okay. We're just waiting for the doctor to come back."

I was happy that I had the support of everyone in the room. But an older, evil-looking nurse quickly came in and killed my vibe.

"I'm sorry but since this is the ER unit, we only allow two people to be back here at a time," she said with a hint of attitude.

Naomi quickly interjected while looking the nurse up and down, "Oh, it's all right. Kenneth and I will go to the waiting area. Come on, hon."

She grabbed him and off they went.

Cameron leaned in closer, taking my hand. "Baby, you okay? I'm so sorry."

"I'm fine, Cameron. No need to be sorry."

We waited for at least twenty minutes before the doctor came in with some news. I was hoping that my physician, Dr. Marabi, was on his way to see me as well. But for now, I was stuck with the ER doctor.

"Hello, you must be Mr. Lewis. I'm Doctor Franklin."

"Nice to meet you, sir," said Cameron, accepting the handshake.

"And this is my friend Alexandra," I interjected.

Alex gave a slight wave as she snapped out of whatever daze she seemed to be in while looking out the window.

"Nice to meet you," the doctor said. "What happened to the others?"

"They had to wait in the waiting area," I said.

Looking very pleasant, the doctor asked, "Well, would you like them to hear the news as well?"

What kind of news did he have?! And was this a trick question?

Confidently, I said, "Sure. I have nothing to hide. Go get them, Cam."

I lay there nervous yet anxious. "Doctor, is the news good or bad? You're making me nervous."

Alex came over and took my hand for comfort.

"Oh, it can go either way," he said.

The three of them came walking through the door.

"Just spit it out, Dr. Franklin," I said.

"Well, we ran tests for your kidneys and abdomen. Everything is normal. Your levels and everything are great."

Cam was getting more anxious than I was. "Okay, and so?!"

The doctor went on. "And so, we also gave you a pregnancy test. I don't know if the two of you were planning to conceive or not."

The room grew tense and quiet.

"You're seven weeks' pregnant."

Naomi screamed out of excitement, and I sat there with my mouth open and eyes wide.

"Oh my goodness, Tan! Congrats!" Alex bent down to hug me.

"I'm going to be a god mommy!" shouted Naomi.

"Oh my gosh, Cameron!" My baby had the biggest grin on his face as he walked over and kissed me.

Everyone expressed their excitement. Things seemed to be going great for us.

CHAPTER 26

~ALEXANDRA~

I could not believe that my girl was two months' pregnant! I was so excited that I had forgotten all about my agreement with Cameron to spill the beans to Tanisha. With the news we had just received, how were we going to reveal *our* news to her?

The doctor had said that Tanisha would not have to stay overnight. So now, we were just waiting for her discharge papers. Naomi and Kenneth had left about an hour ago. I chose to stay for support. When we finally caught a break, Cameron and I stepped in the hallway to consult.

I whispered, "So is our agreement off now because of what happened? Or do you still want to go through with telling her?"

"Alex, I don't know. I mean, we just found out that we're expecting, and that's good news. Telling her now will only make things worse, I think," Cameron said.

Hesitantly, I replied, "I understand. But I—"

"Cameron!" Tanisha called from the room.

"Hold up." Cameron went to go check on his wife.

I didn't want to be the bearer of bad news at a time like this, but something kept urging me to go through with it despite what Cameron wanted.

When I walked back into the room, they both stared at me as if I had some explaining to do.

"What's the matter?" Cameron asked.

"Why don't you tell me?" Tanisha snapped.

Confused, he replied, "I'm not following."

Tanisha paused. "Since we have a bit of time on our hands and the two of you are here, why not just cut to it?"

Uh oh. Where was this coming from?

"Tanisha, what are you talking about?" Cameron stood there as if he had already told her something, like a guilty child who knew they had done something wrong.

Tanisha let it out. "What the hell are the two of you doing behind my back? Ever since I came back from San Diego, neither of you have been yourselves. Cameron's body has been here but his mind is somewhere else. And you have been avoiding me for weeks now. Oh, and the two of you seem to find time to talk all the time when no one's around."

"What are you talking about, baby?"

"I saw your call log, Cameron. What in the world do you and her have to talk about?"

She stared him in the eyes before switching her evil stare over to my direction.

I finally picked up my jaw. "Hold up, so I'm not allowed to talk to your husband without your permission? Since when?"

"You can talk to him all you want. But you know, there's been some shady stuff going on for weeks now and I feel like I'm out of the loop. So why doesn't somebody start talking before I get up out this bed?! Y'all are two of the closest people to me and I know y'all, so trust me, I KNOW WHEN SOMETHING IS UP!"

She didn't have to clap her hands for me to understand she was furious, yet she did.

Cameron threw his hands up and shook his head. Finally, I just blurted it out.

"Cameron and I had sex that night of the party."

"Y'ALL WHAT?!?!" screamed Tanisha.

"Baby, calm down," said Cameron, attempting to hold her down.

"AIN'T NO CALM DOWN NOTHING! GET YOUR HANDS OFF OF ME!"

The nurse quickly came to the rescue. "Is everything all right in here?"

Tanisha replied, "Ma'am, all I ask is that you give me my discharge papers so I can get the hell up outta here before I do something I may regret!"

The nurse quickly scurried out the room with a "Yes ma'am!"

I could see it all over Tanisha's face. She was hot and surely bothered. I looked up to the sky as if looking to God for what to do next. Cameron gave me a conniving look.

"Tan—"

"Ah. Zip it." She threw up her hand. "I don't wanna hear nothing else."

She grabbed her cell phone and called Naomi.

"Hey, I'm sorry to bother you again but do you mind coming to get me? I can't ride home with neither of these two. I might have to kill one of them," she said with a shaky tone.

"Baby, can we just talk?" Cam pleaded.

"I ASKED YOU TO GET YOUR HANDS OFF ME AND I'M NOT GONNA ASK AGAIN!"

The nurse returned with the discharge papers and they began to unhook Tanisha from the monitor.

"Okay, thanks, Naomi. Bye." She began grabbing her belongings.

"Baby, give us a chance to explain. Then you'll understand," said Cameron, still trying.

"Understand what? How my husband slept with my best friend while I was away? What is there to understand?!"

I could tell the young nurse was being nosy and listening to the conversation but I didn't care.

I quickly spoke up. "You'll understand that what happened was a result of us being drunk and that it was never intended. We are sorry, Tanisha."

As she got out the bed, Tanisha said, "Yeah, y'all are sorry, all right. I'll tell y'all what I'm gonna do. Naomi is picking me up and I'll be staying at her place until further notice. Now good night."

Cameron began to beg. "Baby, please don't do that. I need you home with me."

"You'll be fine. Just invite her over if you need company," Tanisha said as the nurse helped her into a wheelchair. "Oh, and thanks for piling bad news on top of my good news. I've had enough shock for one day."

I buried my face in my hands, and the nurse rolled my best friend out the door.

Almost immediately, Cameron scolded me. "I told you, Alex, it wasn't good timing. But you're just gonna have it your way, right?"

Cam shook his head and walked out of the room, leaving me there shallow and all alone. Part of me was upset that

I didn't give it another day, but when I was confronted after walking in the room, I felt I had no choice. The cat was out the bag now and it was up to me to make things right.

Chapter 27

~Naomi~

I arrived at the ER and Tanisha quickly jumped out of her wheelchair and into my car. I thought someone was after her or something. But from the way she sounded on the phone, I knew something was not right.

"Are you okay, Tanisha?"

"Just drive, Naomi."

"What's going on?"

"DRIVE THIS CAR!"

I dropped my jaw and quickly put the car into gear. Either she had just found out about Cameron and Alex or someone in the hospital had tried her. I decided to let her speak when she was ready. Meanwhile, I turned the radio up as my favorite gospel song was playing, "Break Every Chain."

Only a few seconds later, Tanisha snapped, "Can you turn that down? Lord knows I am not in that kind of mood."

I snapped back, "Maybe you need to break a few chains the way you rolled up in my car with all that stank attitude! You hormonal already?"

Tanisha gave me a look that said if I didn't cut the sarcasm, she would be breaking something other than chains.

"Okay, Naomi, do you really want to know what my problem is?"

"Uh, yeah. And why you're not riding home with your husband."

She snapped her fingers as if she had just remembered something. "Oh yeah, speaking of that man, do you mind running me past my house so I can grab a few things? I'll be quick."

I already knew what was up, so I just blurted it out. "You found out about Cam and Alex, huh?"

Tanisha hollered so loud I almost lost control of the car.

"YOU KNEW ABOUT THIS?! OH HELL NO! So now I have TWO shady ass friends AND a cheating husband? I can't deal. Pull this car over!" she demanded.

"Tan, listen to me! Yes, I knew about this. But trust me, I'm not playing sides," I reassured her.

Pissed off, she remarked smartly, "Sure hard to trust anybody these days I tell you!"

As much as I wanted to pull this car over and have a heart to heart with my friend, I knew she was in a rush to beat Cameron home, so I pressed on the gas.

"Look, Tanisha, you have every right to be upset at those two. And even me. But you know something like that couldn't have been planned."

"Well, how long did they *plan* to keep it a secret? Because neither of them would've spoken up if I hadn't called them out on their bull! And how long did you know about this?!"

"I just found out a few days ago. But I encouraged Alex to tell you the truth. I didn't think she would wait until you got the biggest news of your life," I said with a slight chuckle.

"Oh, this takes the win for the biggest news of my life. Nai, I just found out that I will be bringing a life into this world. And on top of that, my husband slept with my best friend! How am I supposed to juggle both of these things at once?"

I could hear the tears coming from her shattered voice.

"With the help of God, you can get through anything. Tan, you know better than anybody how much God loves us and how he wouldn't give us more than we could handle."

"Yeah, but right now I just can't think straight! I feel like this is a joke! Am I being punished and rewarded at the same time?"

I replied, "You know what to do and how to handle this. Don't do anything irrational. Cameron loves you and so does Alex. I'm certain of that. You can't allow this incident to destroy your history with the two. A stupid mistake it was, but you can move past this."

I was hoping my words were hitting the mark somewhere in her brain although I knew she didn't want to hear this right now. But she needed to.

Reluctantly, she said, "Maybe. But I need time."

"Of course. And they have to be willing to give you that time and space. Meanwhile, you can stay at my place until you're good."

"Thanks, Naomi. I know you're right. But right now, I'm just going to focus on myself and this innocent life growing inside of me," Tanisha said.

We pulled up to her house right as the sun went down and she went in to grab her belongings. Meanwhile, I texted Kenneth.

"HAVE TO RESCHEDULE OUR NIGHT TOGETHER. SORRY BAE."

I was slightly upset that I wasn't going to be spending the night with my "boo" because it had been weeks since I had gotten some. But right now, my best friend's well-being was more important.

CHAPTER 28

~TANISHA~

I spent the night at Naomi's place. Luckily she had two bedrooms or else she would've been giving up her bed for a pregnant woman. When I woke up, it dawned on me that I had a child growing inside of me. I was only two months, but it was still good to know the reason for my ongoing pain. I began thinking of Cameron and the awful act he committed. I had a million and one questions in my head. When did they decide to sleep together? Who made the first move? Did they even use a condom? I must've overthought because next thing I knew, I was running to Naomi's bathroom with my head over her sink. If I hadn't found out I was pregnant the day before, this day would've solidified why I wasn't feeling well.

"Tanisha, you okay?" Naomi yelled.

"I'm fine!"

Morning sickness. Ugh. Naomi was in the kitchen fixing breakfast that I may not be able to eat.

I retreated to the bedroom and laid back down.

"Breakfast will be ready in a sec!" she shouted.

I looked at my phone and saw missed calls from both Alexandra and Cameron. I also had about a dozen text messages from Cameron but I had no intentions of reading any of them. He knew where I was and that was all that mattered.

Although I was not at home, I decided to work remotely until next week. I figured I would give myself a few days to clear my head before heading back into the office.

"Come in," I said when Naomi knocked.

"You all right? I heard you make a dash to the bathroom," Naomi asked.

"Yeah, I'm fine. Just morning sickness for the first and probably not last time," I said sarcastically.

Naomi's face lit up. "Ooh, yay! Now it's confirmed you're really pregnant!"

Why was she excited about me throwing up?

"Girl, calm down. Nothing exciting about this crap."

"Okay, you want me to bring you some breakfast?"

"Sure, I'd appreciate that."

She went to get my breakfast and I grabbed my laptop so I could log in and start working.

Cameron called me once again and I didn't bother to answer. But this time, he left a message on my voicemail.

Hey, baby, good morning. I know you don't want to hear from me right now. But I just wanted to let you know that I love you and I want you to have a great day. Take care of our little one as well as yourself. Tell Naomi I said hello. We will talk real soon. I love you with all my heart and I want you to know that I'm truly sorry for how I hurt you.

I rolled my eyes. Naomi walked in with a plate of scrambled eggs, bacon, and toast with a side of applesauce.

"I hope you can eat. Your stomach okay?" she asked.

"Yeah, it's fine. Thanks, girl. Oh, and Cameron said to tell you hello."

"You talked to him?" Her face glowed up.

"Hell no. He left a voicemail just now," I quickly said as I dove into the scrambled eggs.

Naomi laughed. "Just take it one day at a time, girl. I'm gonna go and get dressed for work. You need my car or anything?"

"No, I'm working right here today. You can take your car."

"Okay. I only work a few hours today so I'll be back by three. Call me if you need anything," she said as she walked out the room.

"Thanks, Naomi!"

I appreciated my friend and how she was so willing to take care of me. But I was curious to know if she remembered that I was only two months pregnant and not eight. I was still able to maneuver and do things for myself. But I know she was just being a good friend and that was her nature. I couldn't complain.

I cut the television up, continued eating my breakfast, and tried to focus my mind somewhere else besides my friend and my man.

CHAPTER 29

~ALEXANDRA~

The whole weekend went by and Tanisha was still avoiding my calls. Now I knew firsthand how it felt to be ignored by a friend. I went to church Sunday and Cameron was there but avoided talking to or even looking at me. I felt like it was me against everyone. At least I still had my girl Naomi.

I sat at my desk trying to focus on my work when I heard a knock at the door.

"Come in."

Naomi walked through the door with two Chick-Fil-A bags. My girl!

Quickly taking my attention from my computer, I said, "Naomi! Come through, girlfriend! I knew there was a reason I liked you!"

"Child, please. I'm just doing you a favor. I know you going through it."

She sat down and removed the food from the bags.

It didn't take me long to begin spewing out my emotions. "It hasn't even been a week yet, Nai, and I'm feeling so empty, like I lost my best friend."

Naomi said, "Well, that's normal. But come on, it's not like y'all had some petty fight that can be overlooked. This is something like a big deal."

I munched on the salad she brought me.

"I know that. But it hurts. And to be ignored on top of that?" I questioned with a full mouth.

"Just like you ignored her when you were afraid to speak up?" Naomi fired back.

After a brief silence, I said, "I was never afraid to speak up. I just needed the right opportunity, Nai."

She took a sip of her lemonade.

"There is never a right opportunity to reveal something like that. But that day at the hospital wasn't the right opportunity either," she said.

"I had no choice! She basically cornered Cam and me because she had been suspicious for a while."

"Well, what about Cameron? What does he have to say for himself? I mean, did you or did you not tell me that he initiated the whole thing?" she said with a mouth full of fries.

"Yes, he started the whole thing. But I'm not about pointing fingers at anyone. We both messed up and have to take responsibility. It's only right."

"Mmhmm. I agree," Naomi said.

I sighed. "I just need to talk to her in person so that I can explain how things went down. Do you think she will forgive me?"

Naomi paused for a second.

"Of course I think she will. She's not the person to hold grudges. But you know these things take time, Alex. They don't happen overnight. Give the girl time to process it all. She'll come around."

For once, Naomi was the one giving me advice and it actually made sense. I knew she was right but forgiveness was a thing of patience, which I did not have. I wished that I could go back and erase that entire night from my life.

"Naomi, did I do the right thing by allowing Cameron to come over my place and sober up? I can't help but to think that I caused it all to happen."

She took another sip of lemonade. "Alex, let me tell you something. It wasn't that you did the right or wrong thing. You did what any friend would do. In this situation, Cameron just happens to be your best girl's man, which can be interpreted as you trying to be sneaky behind her back. But since the two of you were highly intoxicated, you did what you felt was best for you and Cameron's safety. Now, Cameron should've done a better job at controlling his urges and keeping his hands to himself. But since you had very little control over him and yourself at the time, it was just the wrong setting to be in. Things happen, Alex. Forgive, let go, and move on. We know there aren't any feelings between the two of you, so stop stressing over it."

Let her be the one to tell it—sex was just a satisfactory release for two individuals. There didn't need to be feelings involved to satisfy a need.

"Oh, just like you and Leon, huh?" I questioned.

"Child, Leon is a thing of the past. My eyes are stuck on Kenneth now. But maybe I should check in on Leon, you know, just to see if anything has changed." Naomi stood up.

I shook my head and laughed. "You are a hot mess, girl."

"Well, so are you. But that's another topic."

"Oh please. But thanks for lunch. I got you next."

"Yeah, you better! I'm going to find my man!" she shouted as she left my office.

I tried to keep my mind off things, so I decided to get back into my paperwork.

Chapter 30

~Naomi~

It had been weeks now since I saw Kenneth. And tonight, he was staying over at my place. After going out to dinner, we decided to settle in and watch a movie.

"Babe, see if Netflix has anything good." I knew Kenneth was into crime and mystery movies, but I was more into romantic ones. Tonight, it was his pick because I really didn't care about the movie. I just wanted to cuddle and get some.

"What about *Blackberry Station*?"

"Sure babe, whatever you want."

He clicked on the movie and it began to play. I could tell already that this was going to be a movie he was actually interested in. *Oh buddy.*

***

An hour and a half later, we were both still up and alert. The movie had turned out to be interesting.

"What you wanna do now?" he asked.

"Let's cuddle."

"Hmm, okay," he answered, unsure.

I was waiting for him to make the first move and at least kiss me. But he was taking too long. Just as I was about to heat things up, he started talking.

"So how long is Tanisha going to stay here?"

"Uh, just a few more days probably. Why?"

"Just asking. I feel bad for her," he said as he rubbed my arm.

"Yeah, me too. But she's strong. She'll be all right."

I slowly reached down to caress him but then he started talking again.

"What do you want out of this, Naomi?"

I hesitated to respond. "Out of what? Us?"

"Yes," he answered sharply.

"Well, I feel like we're good friends right now."

"Yeah, but eventually what do you want from me? What do you want for your future?"

"Honestly, I haven't thought about that. I'm still young so I'm not rushing into anything. Why?" What was with all the questions? Give me sex already!

Kenneth said, "I was just wondering. It's like I'm feeling you more and more each day. But we've only hung out as friends. Yet you keep giving me boyfriend nicknames."

Becoming defensive, I asked, "I'm sorry, do you want me to stop?"

"No, not at all. I don't want to get the wrong impression from you, that's all."

What impression was he getting? This conversation was beginning to take a turn.

"Which is?" I inquired.

"Nothing. Never mind. Let's just go to sleep." He rolled over to try to spoon me.

Sleep? Oh no he did not! First, he ruined my horniness by continuing to talk when I was in the mood. Then, he insinuated something but didn't finish his thoughts. Now he wanted to just go to sleep?!

I released myself from his embrace and said, "Kenneth, you can talk to me."

"I don't want to feel like you just want sex from me."

I sat up in the bed. "Babe, I mean Kenneth, that's not why I want you here. Yeah, I'm excited and like to have sex. But I'm not into you for that. Come on, we've only done it once."

"And how many times have you done it with others?" he asked.

Was he serious right now? I was not in the mood for this bull. Not tonight.

"Really, that's none of your business. I don't question you about who you sleep with and how many times you do it!"

"Okay, Naomi. I guess I'll just remove myself for tonight."

Remove himself? Did he mean he was leaving? "And what exactly does that mean?"

He got up and began to put his shoes on.

"It means I'm not going to argue with you, so I'll just let myself out."

He grabbed his keys and headed for the bedroom door.

"Are you serious, Kenneth? What in the world just happened?"

He stopped and turned to face me. "I asked you a question that you could not give me an answer to."

"Okay, and . . . ? So what? Where did that come from?!"

"Good night, Naomi," he said as he opened the bedroom door and exited my house.

He left me there lost and confused. I couldn't understand why he came at me with all these questions. I was upset and didn't care anymore. Walking over to my dresser, I grabbed my vibrator out of the drawer and hopped back under the covers. This was why I didn't deal with men and relationships. I liked to do me and when they couldn't handle it, it was bye-bye for them.

CHAPTER 31

~TANISHA~

I decided to come back home after three weeks. Although I hadn't talked anything over with my husband or Alex, I wanted to be back in the comfort of my own home. Besides, Cameron was annoying me with his worrying self. He texted me every day to see if the baby and I were doing okay. A few days earlier, Cameron and I went to our first ultrasound. It was so uncomfortable to be around my husband knowing that we were not in tune with one another. We carried on our usual duties but I did everything possible to not have us catch a quiet moment that would open the door for conversation. I still wasn't ready.

I was preparing to leave my office for the day and called Naomi to see what she was up to.

"How are things at home? I'm lonely now since you left me and Kenneth hasn't been coming over," she said.

"Things are stiff at home. I feel like a disoriented couple," I said sadly.

"Aw, I'm sorry, Tan. But at least you are getting back in the swing of things."

"I guess. I just want this to be over with. I miss my husband. I miss my life."

I felt like I was living with a total and complete stranger. Oftentimes I would find myself staring at my husband out of anger when he didn't realize it. I had a million things running around in my brain.

Naomi reminded me, "Forgiveness takes time. Besides, he has to prove that he can earn your trust back."

"You're right. Meanwhile, I'm just praying to God every day to get better."

"You're doing the right thing, my sista. Just keep your head up," she said.

"I will. Thanks, Nai. I'll talk to you later."

Naomi was right. I was trying to figure out why she always had such great advice but she always found herself in compromising situations.

As soon as I hung up my work phone, Alex was calling my cell phone. I was still not answering her calls because I was not ready to talk. No apology given at this moment could make me feel different. I was just hoping that she was learning from her mistakes.

Looking over at our wedding pictures on my desk, I wondered if I had made a mistake marrying Cameron . . . if he really meant the vows he made to me.

CHAPTER 32

~ALEXANDRA~

The weeks went by and I was getting ignored day by day. I was used to it by now but that didn't mean I enjoyed it. To keep my focus off my diminishing friendship, I got involved with the church's volunteer program. On this day, we were distributing care packages to the homeless at a nearby shelter. I decided that my weekends would be dedicated to giving my time and help to those in need. I was realizing that there were more important things going on in the world and that I shouldn't be weighed down by the actions of others. Yes, I wanted to restore my friendship with Tanisha. But I couldn't rush her. Instead, I had to pray about it.

"Sister Moore, how nice to see you out here today," the pastor said.

"Yes Pastor, the Lord has been speaking to me through your sermons. It's not about me; it's about Him."

"That's right," he said. "And God has called us as His servants to do all that we can for the less fortunate. I'm glad to see you."

"Thanks, Pastor."

I walked over to one of the ladies who appeared to be around my age if not younger. She caught my attention with her frizzy hair and shaggy clothes. But her face was so pretty that she could've been featured on a magazine cover.

"Hi, my name is Alexandra," I said, extending my hand.

She looked at me for a second before saying "Hi," then looked at my hand.

I asked, "What's your name?"

"Bridget," she answered sourly.

"Hello, Bridget. How are you today?"

"Not so good."

I didn't want to press her but in my spirit, I felt she had something she needed to get off her chest.

"If you don't mind me asking, what's wrong?"

"You wouldn't understand," Bridget said.

"Try me."

She hesitated, then began to unfold.

"I don't have enough money for next month's rent. I live in a neighborhood down the street for low income people. I don't know where my kids and I are going to go."

Wow. I felt for this young lady. "Can I ask how old you are?"

"I'm twenty-three."

"Oh Bridget, I'm so sorry."

"I come to this shelter every month when your church gives out care packages. It really helps my children out. I don't get any assistance from my family. They don't want to have anything to do with me," Bridget went on.

"Why not?"

"When I first got pregnant at seventeen, I decided to move out of my mom's house and live with my boyfriend. He got locked up after the first year of my daughter's life, and ever since then, my mom's bashed me for being fast and she's had nothing to do with me."

I made a startling suggestion. "Have you ever thought about coming to our church, Temple of Hope? You know, there are programs that can help you."

Bridget answered, "I rarely have time. I work three jobs and in between, I'm trying to make sure my kids have what they need. But I just got laid off from one of my jobs, which is why I will be short for next month's rent."

Poor child. I wanted to help this girl out financially, and I could have with the kind of money that I brought home. But the spirit didn't say to move in that direction.

"Wow, Bridget. Things will get better. But maybe I can put you in contact with someone from the church who can assist you."

"That would be nice," she said with a smile.

I pulled out one of our church's brochures. "Our pastor's number and the church's number is on here. Just call. Would you like to meet the pastor right now?"

"Umm, not now. I have to go drop this stuff off so I can get to work. But I'll call. Thank you. Alex, right?"

"Yes, Alex. Nice to meet you, Bridget."

"Okay, you too." She waved as she walked away.

My first time volunteering with the church and I had already helped out more than I expected to. Perhaps this was my calling. Bridget seemed like a smart girl. I just hoped that she would use that number.

CHAPTER 33

~NAOMI~

Kenneth and I hadn't spoken in a week. Yes, I missed him and I wanted to talk to him. But I did not want to be the one to make the first move. It was my first weekend hanging alone since Kenneth and I seemed to have gotten closer. I was bored and nothing good was on my television, so there I sat flipping channels and stuffing my belly with chips. Giving Kenneth time and space, I decided to check on Leon to get an update on how his relationship was doing.

"Well, Melissa and I are still about the same. We tried to talk but it's like it goes in one ear and out the other," Leon said.

"Mmm. I don't know what to tell you, Leon. I really hope she comes around."

"Yeah, so do I. Hopefully before it's too late. So what's up with you?"

"Uh, nothing I guess," I replied, trying to sound casual and unbothered.

"Really? C'mon, Naomi, there's always something going on with you. Have you settled down yet?"

Ew, why was Leon interested in my personal business? Since when did he care about what I did?

I replied, "No I have not settled down with anyone. I'm not sure that's going to happen anytime soon."

"And why not?"

"Because dudes are foul and they can't handle me," I answered, rolling my eyes.

"Oh well, excuse me then."

I didn't want to talk to Leon about Kenneth, but maybe it wouldn't hurt hearing things from a man's perspective. "Leon, what would you do if you felt a woman just wanted you for sex?"

He responded, "Whoa, I never thought about that. Hmm. Honestly, I'd probably leave her."

I dropped my jaw full of chips and put the phone down for a second.

"You there, Naomi?"

"Yeah, I'm here. I was just shocked by your answer."

"Why? I mean, think of it the opposite way. Would you feel comfortable if all a guy wanted from you was what was underneath your clothes? People have to bring more to the table than just sex. Wouldn't you agree?"

"I agree. It's just that somehow this guy that I'm talking to is under the impression that that's all I want from him. And it's not true."

Leon went on, "Hmm. Well, take it from me. Guys like sex. But it can be offensive if that is all a woman wants from us. How did he get that vibe?"

"I don't know! I've only slept with him once!"

I couldn't believe that I was being an open book with Leon. But for some reason, I respected his advice.

"Maybe he's guilty of something or just used to a woman wanting him for his goods," he suggested.

"Well what do you suggest I do?"

"Just tell him how you really feel. Maybe it's an honest misunderstanding. If he's feeling you as a person, then what's meant to be will happen."

I hated to admit it, but Leon's advice made sense. I just had to clear things up with Kenneth and get him to understand that I was not like other chicks he may have dated. I had no issue speaking up for myself and letting my desires be known. Maybe this was something he was not used to.

"Thanks, Leon, you're all right with me." I smiled, still munching on snacks.

"I don't mind helping those who help me."

CHAPTER 34

~TANISHA~

This pregnancy was going by way too fast for me to keep up! I was already five months in and of course I had started showing. What was meant to be a secret was slowly unfolding to everyone, especially the members at the church. But this particular Sunday, something spoke to my heart. The pastor preached about forgiveness and the fact that if Jesus was able to die for us and forgives us for our sins, then we should be able to do the same for one another. That's when the Lord revealed to me that it was time to confront the situation that I had been avoiding. I invited Alex to come over after church so that the three of us could sit and talk. I still was resistant to talking, but I was sure that the Holy Spirit would speak for me.

When the doorbell rang, I hollered for Cam to get the door.

It was Alex. She joined me on the patio. Alex and I hadn't spoken face-to-face since being at the hospital three months ago. And whenever I'd see her at church, I would quickly divert my attention to something else.

"Hello. Tanisha."

"Hi, Alex, come and sit down," I instructed her.

I could tell she was uneasy because she didn't know what to expect.

"Have you eaten?" I inquired. Poor girl was probably too nervous to eat.

"Yeah, I grabbed something after church. But I'll take a water please."

I got up and grabbed a bottle of water from my fridge. Cameron joined us.

There was silence between the three of us, so I took the lead.

"So, we all know why we're here. Let's get to it. Um, I know that this has not been easy for any of us. But I do need clarity. I can't keep living like this. I'm halfway through my pregnancy and it's like my husband and I are not on the same page nor is my friendship with you, Alex."

"Baby, let me say this," Cam interjected. "First of all, I am deeply sorry for what I have done to you. I apologize to you every day and I mean it each time. Anything you want to discuss, I will. There are no secrets at this table."

Alex looked uncomfortable but she knew what time it was. "Tanisha, I, too, am sorry for what this has done to you. I pray every day that you will forgive me and us because I know that we can overcome this."

I was over their apologies. I wanted them to start confessing to what it was that they did. I needed answers!

"You guys, I need the truth to come out. Was this an ongoing thing? How many times? Why for goodness sake?!" I asked.

Alex took the lead.

"That night, Cameron and I were both extremely drunk. I didn't drive so Cameron offered to drop me off at home but he was really bad. So, I drove us to my place thinking that he would sober up and leave by morning."

Cameron insisted on finishing the story.

"And I made a move on Alex. Looking back on it, I couldn't control myself, Tanisha. And for the record, I don't look at Alex in that way. But she was trying to be a good friend and help me out. I took advantage of her friendship and loyalty to you and I'm sorry."

Alex jumped in.

"This was a one-time thing that I promise you will NEVER happen again."

I had plenty of other questions, but the main thing I wanted to know had to be thrown out on the table . . . After a brief pause, I let it out. "Did you two use protection that night?"

They both were silent and looked at one another. I'm not even sure if they remembered or not. That's when the tears started falling from my face and I got up to excuse myself from the table.

"Baby, please come back," Cam said as he tried to grab me.

I went into the hallway bathroom and locked the door behind me. I sobbed as I looked at myself in the mirror. I was beginning to have suspicions again. What if they didn't use protection? What if this whole scenario was made up? How could I ever trust my husband and my best friend again?

CHAPTER 35

~ALEXANDRA~

I felt so bad knowing that Cameron and I couldn't give Tanisha a direct answer. I was pretty sure that we did not use protection. Tanisha was still in the bathroom and Cameron had gone to try to talk her into coming out so we could finish the conversation. Meanwhile, I got a call from Pastor Henderson.

"Hello, Pastor!" I attempted to sound jolly despite the condition I was in.

"Alexandra, how are you, my dear?"

"I'm doing well." I couldn't help but wonder why he was calling me on a Sunday evening.

"I did not get a chance to catch you after service, but I wanted to pass on some good news," Pastor Henderson said.

"I'm listening, sir."

"Well, you remember a few months ago when we went to give out our care packages down at the shelter?"

"Yes, like we do every month."

"I talked to a young lady named Bridget this weekend. She gave me your name and said that you referred her to our church."

"Yes, I did. I haven't seen her for the past two months. Is she all right?"

"Well, she asked how she could receive assistance because she is in a tough spot right now. I set it up so that our Christian caring ministry can help her out with this month's rent. Ain't that good news!" Pastor Henderson exclaimed.

That was excellent news!

"I'm excited to hear that, Pastor, but she told me two months ago that she didn't know how she was going to get by for rent that next month. Where did she stay for two months?"

"She and her kids had to go stay at a shelter," he replied sourly.

Wow. Why didn't she use the resources I extended to her two months earlier? But it was never too late.

Pastor Henderson continued, "I just wanted to let you know this, Alex, not because she gave me your name but because I have witnessed firsthand how you allow your light to shine through others. I really admire that and I know that God is pleased."

"Why thank you so much, Pastor. I'm glad to be a vessel for the Lord," I said with a half smile.

"All right now, you enjoy your Sunday evening. Or what's left of it."

"Okay, you too now," I said and hung up.

I was ecstatic that Bridget finally gave in and allowed someone to help her out in her time of need. I was also hoping that she would return to the food shelter next month and eventually come and visit our church. It felt good to hear something positive was happening that I played a part in. But I couldn't forget that quickly where I was sitting and why.

CHAPTER 36

~NAOMI~

It had been two months since Kenneth and I had seen each other. And now he was at my place, sitting in my living room. I had missed him, but he and I both knew that we had some things to talk about. After fixing us a quick snack, I joined him on the couch.

"Kenneth, where have you been?" I asked casually.

"I've been doing me. Taking some time to evaluate things, that's all."

He was so nonchalant about it.

"And what exactly did you evaluate?"

"You . . . Me . . . Us."

If he had plans to leave me after all this time, I wish he'd just say it already.

Still probing, I asked, "And?"

"And, I realize that I want what's best for the both of us. Truth is, I love you, Naomi. I want this to work."

I couldn't do anything but sit there. Did he just say he loved me? This was definitely something I was not used to hearing. I was speechless! I jumped on Kenneth's lap and gave him the biggest hug.

"Bae, you okay?" he asked, unprepared to catch me with open arms.

"Yes, just hug me!"

I was so certain that he would be leaving my pitiful behind. But look at God.

"Kenneth, I thought you were going to break things off with me."

"What? Why would I do that? I just needed time to think."

"I know, but when you left, you left with the notion that I wanted you for all the wrong reasons. I want you to be certain that I love you and want you for so much more than that."

"Nai, you've told me about your past. I respect all that you went through. But I am willing to be patient with you and give us a chance. We'll never know if we don't try, right?" he said, gazing into my eyes.

"Right, baby," I replied.

We kissed for the first time in two months. God I missed his soft, luscious lips. I know that he said he needed time to process us, but two months was a long time to be silent with someone you supposedly love. Although we weren't fully committed to one another, I knew that I had been faithful in those two months and I was praying that Kenneth was the same.

Feeling relieved, I said, "Whew, I did not expect this to be so simple. I mean, really, Kenneth."

"Well, it is. Love is simple. I love you."

He started kissing me in all the right places, hinting that he wanted to take this to the bedroom.

"Mmm, babe, let's not do that tonight," I suggested.

He paused and looked at me.

"You're kidding, right?"

"No, I'm not," I said with a straight face.

This was so hard because as tempted as I was, I felt inclined to resist. But it was all part of my plan.

"Why not? What's wrong?" he asked.

"Nothing, I just want to enjoy your company."

Lord knows I was itching for some intimacy. But I wanted to prove to Kenneth that I could spend innocent time with him without sex. I knew he was upset and secretly so was I. But I was changing for all the right reasons.

With me still sitting in his arms, he sat up and said, "Baby, we haven't been intimate in over two months. How much longer do you expect me to hold out?!"

I kissed his soft lips and turned on the television.

I could tell he wasn't thrilled about my decision. But I smiled because it felt good to have my man right back where I wanted him.

CHAPTER 37

~TANISHA~

"Baby, you okay?" Cameron knocked on the bathroom door.

I pulled myself together and slowly opened the door. There Cameron stood with disappointment and worry written all over his face.

"Tan, I don't know what to say."

Of course he didn't. Clearly Alex didn't know either.

"Let's just go back out here and settle this once and for all," I said with slight saltiness in my tone.

We joined Alex on the patio. She had just wrapped up a phone call.

Continuing where we left off, I said, "Ahem. Well, since neither of you knows the answer to the million-dollar question, I'm just going to say one thing—"

"We didn't," Alex said, abrasively cutting me off mid-sentence.

"What?" I exclaimed.

"We didn't use protection that night."

I had finally received an answer but of course it was not the answer I wanted to hear. It took everything in me to stay put in my seat because I wanted to jump across the table and go Crenshaw Heights on the both of them.

"Baby, we went and got tested to make sure we were straight," Cameron said.

"And that makes it all okay, huh?" Tears began to fall from my eyes again.

"Well, no Tanisha. But at least we both know we are clear," Alex said.

I had to ask.

"You two went together?"

"No baby, we didn't," answered Cameron.

I felt like I was back at square one. But I stood strong at the pastor's message from that morning about forgiveness. I knew in my heart that it was the right thing to forgive them, but that didn't mean I had to forget.

Despite my feelings of betrayal, I had to think about the next step after forgiveness. Should I move on and act like things are normal? I had to be honest with myself. I never considered divorce months into my marriage as an option, but how would I feel being with this man I couldn't fully trust?

How would I sit with Alex and look her in the eyes knowing that she slept with my husband? Trust was a huge deal on both parties and I didn't know which direction to go.

After a deep sigh, I said, "All I'm going to say is . . . that I forgive you. I forgive what you two did but rest assured, I will never forget. As far as what goes on from here, only God knows because I don't. But I wanted to have this talk to clear the barrier and to lift a burden from my heart."

"Thank you for your forgiveness, Tanisha. I promise from here on out that you will again be able to trust me," Alex said as she stood to hug me. "I'm sorry but I have to go. I'm so glad we were all able to have this conversation. I'll text you later, Tan, okay?"

"Yeah, sure," I replied stiffly. I couldn't even look at her.

Alex let herself out, and Cameron pulled his chair closer to mine and looked into my eyes.

"Baby, I, too, thank you for forgiving me. I know we're gonna overcome this," he said.

I gave him a stern look. He took my hands and bowed his head. As he began to pray, I focused on my husband's demeanor. In my heart I knew that he really was sorry and that he wanted us back on the same page. I bowed my head and joined him.

" . . . Oh heavenly father, I know there was a reason for us being together but I'm asking You to remain at the center of this household. Thank You for forgiveness, Father. In Jesus' name, amen."

"Amen," I said.

We hugged one another as the tears still fell silently down my cheeks.

"I love you, Cameron," I whispered.

"I love you too, Tanisha."

Step one to forgiveness was complete.

CHAPTER 38

~ALEXANDRA~

I was so happy that Tanisha had decided to forgive me. After all that time, I wasn't so sure if we were ever going to be friends again. But things seemed to be looking up lately. As I was sitting on my couch reading a book, my cell phone rang. Across the screen appeared Pastor Henderson's name. I turned the volume down on the television and picked up the call.

"Hello, Pastor!"

"Hey, Sister Alexandra, how are ya?"

"I'm well, sir. And you?"

"Ah, I'm doing just fine. Do you have a minute? I wanted to run something by you that the Lord has placed on my heart," he said.

I was most certain that he had in mind a new task for me to do. I wondered what it was this time.

Intrigued, I asked, "Okay, what's that?"

"Alex, let me start by saying that I admire your passion and eagerness to learn. I notice you come to Bible study during the week and are quite active in your Sunday school class."

Uh oh. Was he hinting at me to become a Sunday school teacher?

"Yes Pastor Henderson, I enjoy learning," I said passionately.

"Well, amen. Alexandra, have you ever considered ministry?"

Now smiling, I replied, "Well, yes sir. You already know I'm a part of the Hope ministry. I love giving out those packages once a month."

"Yes." He chuckled. "But that's not exactly what I meant. I'm talking about becoming an ordained minister of the gospel."

"A preacher?!"

"Yes Alexandra, a minister."

Out of all the callings in life, I never imagined that preaching would be mine. This prophecy took me by surprise. After a few seconds of awkward silence, Pastor Henderson spoke up.

"You there, sister?"

"Yes, I'm here. And I'm sorry for screaming in your ear. That was rude of me."

"It's okay. You know, it has been my vision to restore the young adult ministry, and this might be the year seeing as though we recently have attracted a number of young adults who have been visiting. Now look, Alex, I'm not trying to push you into anything that you or the Lord does not see fit to happen. But it's just a consideration. Pray on it, give it some time. Just know that whatever you decide, I'm fine with it," Pastor Henderson said.

I sat there frozen in my seat. The pastor had given me a lot to think about.

"Wow sir," I said nervously, "I will pray about this. I've had a lot take place in my life over the past few months. This is a surprise. You have to imagine how I'm feeling right now."

"Oh yes, I know it's a lot and I didn't mean to frighten you. But as I said, the Lord placed you upon my heart. But if He doesn't do the same for you, then there is always room in other areas of the church. Now, you have a good rest of the day, Alex. All right?"

"Yes sir, thank you. You too," I replied and hung up.

I couldn't believe what I had just heard. I could not understand why the Lord placed me on Pastor's heart especially at a time like this, when I was just at the brink of getting my life back on track. Alexandra Moore? A minister? All I could do was pray about it and eventually make my decision.

CHAPTER 39

~NAOMI~

Three months later, after our two-month hiatus, my relationship with Kenneth was turning out to be something I never expected for myself. Here I was, happy in love. Kenneth treated me in a way I'd never been treated before—like a man should when he loves a woman. I felt like I was finally into someone for all the right reasons and I was starting to discover what the definition of true love meant.

With my best friend being married and now eight months pregnant, I felt like I was behind. Alex and I had planned a baby shower for Tanisha and Cameron. Her pregnancy seemed to be going by so fast, I was certain that I couldn't keep up.

Alex and I met up at my place to finalize the baby shower plans.

While unpacking some materials, I asked, "Alex, I never understood why couples want to be surprised finding out the sex of their baby. Wouldn't you want to know what you were having as soon as you could?"

Alex replied, "Honestly, I wouldn't mind either way. As long as my baby is growing healthy inside of me, that's all that matters."

Putting together a baby shower was exciting. And this particular one was even more exciting because it was both a gender reveal and shower all in one. Only Alex and I knew if the baby was a boy or girl.

"I hear you. But I want to know what I'm having the first chance I get! Who do you think is gonna have a baby first, Alex, you or me?" I asked.

She burst out laughing.

"Nai, we all know it will be you. Besides, you're the one who's madly in love." She drew an imaginary heart in the sky.

"You might be right about that."

I didn't understand how Alex was so comfortable being single. But I figured her time would come, hopefully sooner rather than later. Then a thought popped in my head.

"Alex, I know exactly what to do with you. I'm going to set you up on a blind date!"

Confused and startled, Alex responded, "Huh? Oh no, you tripping, girlfriend. I don't need no date. I can manage by myself."

"Yeah, you managing, all right. But what's wrong with a lil boy toy in ya life? What could go wrong?"

"Naomi, if I were to ever let anybody set me up for a blind date, the last person would be you! You'd have me going out with some ole sugar daddy type of guy," she said.

"Hell, what's wrong with that?! You can get pleasured and financed at the same time!"

We both laughed.

As Alex and I were still trying to assemble a few decorations for the shower, I got a phone call.

"Tan? What's up, girl? Alex and I are sitting here—"

I couldn't finish my sentence before Cameron was telling me that he and Tanisha were at the hospital.

CHAPTER 40

~TANISHA~

Here I was at the hospital yet again. The last time I was here six months ago, I found out that I was pregnant. This time, I was having complications with my pregnancy. I was so nervous but thank God that Cameron was by my side.

Naomi, Alex, and Cameron entered my room, and Cameron walked up and kissed my forehead. "Baby, are you all right?"

"Yes, I'm fine now," I replied.

"Tanisha!" Naomi exclaimed, as she and Alex gave me a hug. "You had us so worried, girl!"

"I'll be fine. I just want my baby to be okay."

"And he or she will be!" assured Cameron.

The doctor walked in just in time for an update.

"Hello, I'm Dr. Marabi. It's nice to see you all but unfortunate under these circumstances."

"What do you mean, Doctor?" I asked.

"Well, your placenta has partially abrupted, which is why you were bleeding. In order to fix that, we will have to do an emergency C-section."

"This early?" Naomi asked.

"Yes. Tanisha is thirty-three weeks pregnant, which would be considered a preterm labor. But from the ultrasound, her baby is doing just fine," Dr. Marabi said with a pleasant tone.

Cameron looked worried and upset. "Doc, is there a way we can delay her labor?"

"I can give corticosteroids to your wife to prevent the baby from developing any conditions and to speed up its development. But if we want to avoid her placenta completely abrupting, we should act fast. The baby would be in the NICU for a few weeks, but I'm most certain that he, ahem, or she will be just fine."

"Cam, baby, what do you want to do?" I asked, looking him in his eyes.

It was up to my husband to decide what was best for us. Since my pain was past level ten and to avoid any more bleeding, I wanted to deliver the baby immediately and I believe Cameron knew that just from the look in my eyes.

"I say we get this C-section. Let's have at it, Doc," he said.

"Very well. I'll get you transferred to our labor and delivery unit." Dr. Marabi left the room.

I cried out, "You guys, I am in so much pain."

"Tan, it's going to be all right. Just try to relax and stay calm. We're here all the way," Alex said.

"I appreciate you guys. OH NO!" I yelled.

"WHAT?!" everyone exclaimed.

I brought my voice back down. "What about the baby shower?!"

It had just dawned on me that I didn't plan to find out the gender of my baby until my reveal. But with current events, I'd be finding out the sex in a few minutes.

"Don't worry about it, Tan. We'll still have a shower; you just won't be surprised by the gender," Naomi said.

"You ladies are the best. You are too much for words!" I said, now feeling assured.

Once again, my contractions were starting back up. But thankfully the nurses were coming in to wheel me to the delivery unit.

"Ahhhh, Cameron! It hurts so bad!"

"I'm here for you, baby!" he said, holding my hand as I was being wheeled out.

"We'll be waiting for you guys up in the waiting area! You got this, Tanisha!" Alex yelled.

"We love you!" Naomi yelled right behind her.

I was so thankful for the love and support from my best friends. But I was also nervous about delivering my baby prematurely. Somehow I felt assured knowing that God had a purpose, and I was relying on Him to get me, Cameron, and our baby through this.

CHAPTER 41

~ALEXANDRA~

Sitting with Naomi in the waiting room of the delivery unit, I had imagined this moment in my dreams but not in this way. Our best friend was in the process of delivering her baby and I sat there so calmly. Everyone was nervous except me. I knew that everything was going to be okay and that Tanisha would deliver a nice healthy baby.

"So much for the gender reveal, huh?" I said to Naomi.

"Yeah. But it wasn't a reveal for us," Naomi said. "I say we go through with the shower, even if not everyone shows. Especially since most of what we have is nonrefundable." She laughed.

"I'm with you," I concurred.

We sat there in silence for a few minutes.

"Nai, what do you think about me ministering?"

"Uh, like in dance or something?" she asked seriously.

"No girl! Like preaching!"

I didn't get the reaction I thought I would. Instead of bursting out laughing like I did, Naomi stared at me with a slight grin on her face.

"You serious?" she asked.

"Yeah. What would you think?"

"Hmm. I think that would be something nice," she said with a now complete smile.

I couldn't believe my ears.

"Really, Nai?"

"Mmhmm. I mean, you already are intrigued by the word. You know your stuff, Alex. But who planted this in your head?"

Aah, finally. I was waiting for her to ask.

"Well, Pastor Henderson mentioned it to me a few months ago. He told me to think about it."

"Girl, why didn't you say anything sooner? Doesn't he need an answer like yesterday?"

"Well, that's the thing. It's been three months since he's asked. It's not like he gave me a deadline or anything, but I've been praying and fasting about it."

"And what did the Lord say, girl?" Naomi reminded me of a hood Christian if there were such a thing.

"I believe it's what He wants me to do. I mean, I can't deny what God has planned for me, right?"

"Well, yeah, but had it ever crossed your mind before the pastor mentioned it?"

Naomi was playing investigator.

"Honestly, no. But we never know what God has planned for us, right?" I asked, sounding a bit unsure.

Naomi went on. "Right, girl. I just hope Pastor doesn't come to me next, prophesying that I'm supposed to be doing something in the church, because Lord knows . . . "

Naomi was a trip. She was a C-M-E churchgoer, mainly attending on special holidays and rarely every Sunday.

"Have you mentioned this to Tanisha?" she asked.

"No, not anyone but you."

"You and these secrets, girl," Naomi said with a smack of the teeth.

"Nai, it's not a secret!" I said, giving her a slap on her shoulder.

"Okay, so how come you told me and not your other best friend?"

"Because I needed to process it, for one. Two, between putting together the baby shower and work, I haven't had time. I was going to tell you both together!" I hollered loud enough for only her to hear.

"Hmm. Well, I won't share your good news with Tanisha. I'll let you do the honors, ma'am."

"Thank you," I said, sitting back in my chair.

Naomi's phone rang. I swear, she had a hotline all the time.

"Hold on, girl, this is Kenneth." She walked over to the nearby window to take the call.

A second later, the nurse came and informed us that Tanisha had delivered her baby. I motioned for Naomi to come on and she gave me the "in-a-minute" finger. I couldn't wait to see the blessing the Lord had delivered unto my best friend.

CHAPTER 42

~NAOMI~

"Bae? Why you sound upset? Everything okay?" I asked Kenneth when he called.

"My pops died, Nai."

I took a seat as I felt my knees becoming weak. I was getting good news from one place and bad news from another.

"Your dad? My goodness, bae. I'm soooo sorry."

"He had a heart attack," Kenneth replied somberly.

"Are you all right? Where are you?"

"I'll be fine. Don't worry. I'm at home," he said.

"Okay, I'll be there in half an hour. Just let me go see Tanisha and the baby and I'll be there."

"Babe, you don't have to do that. You should be there for your friend. I told you, I'm good."

He was tripping. It was possible for me to be there for two of the people I loved at the same time.

"Kenneth, I said I'll be there in thirty. I love you."

I hung up the phone and rushed to catch up with Alex, who had just entered Tanisha's room.

"Where's the baby?" I asked, expecting to see Tanisha holding her child in her arms like any other mom would do after just giving birth.

Tanisha responded in a rough tone. "They had to take him to the NICU, Nai."

"Well, was he breathing okay and everything?! Y'all got me worried now!"

Cameron jumped up from his seat. "Everything's okay, Naomi. His breathing was a little off since he's here a bit early. But the nurses said he'll be all right. We can see him in a few."

"Oh, right," I said calmly.

How silly of me to forget that quick that the little man was entering the world a bit earlier than we expected. But I guess my mind was on Kenneth.

"You guys, I really want to stay here with you. But Kenneth called me with some not-so-great news," I shared.

"What's wrong?" cried Alex.

I took a deep breath. "Uh, he said his dad had a heart attack. He's dead."

The minute I said that, I couldn't help but let the tears fall.

"Oh Nai." Alex wrapped her arms around me.

I thought I wouldn't have cried until I got to Kenneth's side, but who was I kidding. I was a big emotional baby.

"Nai, I'm sorry to hear that. You go ahead and go see Kenneth; I totally understand," Tanisha said.

"Really? But I want to see the baby," I said while wiping my tears of excitement and sadness.

"You will . . . eventually. Just go take care of business right now," Cameron said.

And I did just that.

Thirty minutes later like I promised, I was at Kenneth's place. Although he wasn't acting sad, I could tell that he was not himself. I wanted to give him his space but I also wanted to remain close and remind him that I was by his side.

I quickly switched into girlfriend mode, attempting to take care of my man. I didn't know how to be helpful in these kinds of situations.

"Did you eat anything?" I asked.

"No."

"Are you hungry?"

"No."

The silence and one-word answers bothered me.

"Do you want to talk?"

"Not right now."

He just sat there watching TV. I didn't know what to do, so I sat there on my phone, surfing my social media.

Kenneth's cell rang and he got up and went to another room to take the call.

Hmmm.

So much for rushing here for this, I thought. Part of me felt like I should have just remained at the hospital with Tanisha. I didn't seem to be doing much by being here. My presence didn't seem to matter to him. I knew that the news was fresh and that people grieve in different ways. But I sure was not used to this.

CHAPTER 43

~TANISHA~

My doctor had informed me that I would be discharged from the hospital in a few hours. I was excited of course, but sad that I would not be bringing baby boy home with us. By now, Alex had left, so it was just Cameron and me.

"Cameron, we have to decide on a name for the baby."

"I know, baby, but I feel like I have to see him first."

"Of course," I said with a grin.

Cameron and I had discussed baby names throughout the last few weeks. But without knowing the sex of our baby, it was a party between the two of us blurting out both girls and boys names.

"Cam, I'm so upset that the girls put all that work into the baby shower. I swear, if I knew this was going to happen—"

"Babe." Cam quickly cut me off and took my hand. "There's no way any of us would have known anything. You never know what to expect with pregnancies. Just be grateful that he's here and doing well. Besides, we can still have the shower as planned."

"You're right, honey."

After my husband gave me the reminder I so desperately needed, my nurse walked in with good news.

"Are Mom and Dad ready to visit baby boy in the NICU?"

A huge grin spread across my face as I wiped away tears. "YES! YES!"

I almost jumped out of that hospital bed.

"Calm down, babe!" Cam said.

The nurse giggled. "Well, let's go!"

As I was being wheeled to the NICU, I praised and thanked God for allowing my son to be delivered without massive complications. I was slightly feeling better, but I knew that after viewing my son for the first time in some hours, I would feel a whole lot better.

"Okay, we're here. You two take as much time as you need. I'll be waiting outside," the nurse said.

"Thank you, Melissa," I replied.

"Ready, babe?" Cam said.

"Oh, I *been* ready!"

We entered the NICU and I couldn't help but notice all the other babies hooked up to machines, some appearing to be lifeless and others squirming and crying. It was an emotional sight. But when Cam and I walked up on our child, I smiled and cried happy tears. There he was, small and frail. He had movement in his limbs yet his eyes remained closed. We cleansed our hands and Cameron opened the incubator. I touched my baby's tiny fingers and he instantly curled his fingers around my one.

"Hi baby, it's your mommy," I whispered.

"Aw, Tanisha, he's so handsome already," said Cameron.

"And he has your nose, babe."

Our little trooper slowly opened his eyes and looked straight at his daddy.

"Hey, lil man. Dad's here too," Cam assured.

Cameron touched his fingers along with mine.

"Any names brewing in that head of yours yet, Daddy?"

He answered, "A couple."

I had a few in my head as well. I was sure that we would agree on something before we left baby boy.

CHAPTER 44

~ALEXANDRA~

I knew time was ticking. Pastor Henderson was waiting for my answer and although he hadn't given me a deadline, I didn't like to keep folks waiting. After praying and fasting for three months, I believed that I had my answer. I picked up the phone to call my pastor but before I could dial, I had an incoming call. It was Tanisha.

"Alex! What's going on?"

"Nothing much. What's up with you?"

"I just wanted you to know that I'm going home tonight."

"That's great news, girl! What about the baby?" I asked.

"He'll be coming home in a few weeks, they said."

"Oh sorry to hear that. But praise God he's all right. You two decide on a name yet?"

"We did actually. It's Joshua," she said.

"Aw! Little Josh!" I said with a huge grin.

I was so happy for my best friend. What a special name for a precious baby. I still couldn't wait to meet him.

"Yep, my courageous little Joshua. Just can't wait for him to join us at home."

"Don't worry, Tan, it won't be long before he does. You got a minute?"

"Yeah, what's up?"

I figured I'd tell Tanisha about the whole minister gig before Naomi blabbed.

"So what do you think about me becoming a minister?"

"Is that a trick question?" Tanisha asked.

I laughed.

"No, just wondering how you'd feel."

"I think it's great!"

"Yeah? Well, so does Pastor."

"I respect Pastor Henderson," Tanisha said. "Not just because he's a pastor but because he keeps it real! And if he placed that on your heart, then you know it's not his doing!"

I was so happy to receive positive feedback from both of my girls about something like this. Now that I had an extra boost, I knew for sure that I was ready to climb onboard.

"I'm glad to hear you say that, Tanisha. I was actually about to call him and give him my answer."

"Well, don't let me hold you, Alex. And tell him I said hello, will ya?!"

I said, "Sure thing. Call me tonight when you get home."

I didn't inform my friends about this opportunity for validation. But the added support was definitely welcome. I was no longer nervous about the whole thing. Excitement filled my heart as I dialed the pastor's number.

"Pastor Henderson? I have an answer."

CHAPTER 45

~NAOMI~

A week had passed by already and it was the day of the funeral. This had to be one of the most stressful weeks of my life. Being by Kenneth's side and helping to make arrangements really took its toll on me. It also didn't help that Kenneth had a solitary attitude. After all, he did just lose his father. Why couldn't I understand that?

After the opening selection, "Near the Cross," many of the congregants were wiping tears from their faces. We were only a few minutes into the service and the sanctuary was already overflowing. As I stood in the rear of the church making sure everything was going smoothly, in walked Alex and Tanisha. I hugged them and motioned for them to sit a couple of rows ahead.

I wanted to go and sit with Kenneth to be moral support. But with his attitude, I thought it was best for me to stay out of the way.

A second later, I raised my head to see Kenneth heading in my direction.

"You all right, baby?" I asked him.

"Yeah, aren't you coming to sit with me?"

"You know, I was just making sure everything was in place back here, keeping things running smoothly."

"I appreciate that. But you should come sit down."

I gave in and said, "Well, all right."

Tanisha and Alex gave me that look as if I were in trouble.

After we took our front row seats, the minister continued along with the program.

"We will now have a selection from our choir."

Funerals could be so depressing and solemn, but if the choir sang an upbeat selection, it made things a bit better. They broke out singing a fast rendition of "Blessed Assurance," which had me standing on my feet clapping my hands. Poor Kenneth remained in his seat with his head down.

***

At the repast located in the church's lower level, so many family and friends gathered together. It sort of felt like a family reunion. I just wasn't a part of the family yet.

While Kenneth embraced many of his family members, I thought it was my chance to branch off and catch up with my girls. I joined Alex and Tanisha at their table.

"Ladies, a beautiful service, was it not?" I asked as I grabbed a seat.

"The minister delivered an on-time sermon," said Alex, the minister-in-training.

"Yeah, it was good," Tanisha chimed in.

I said, "I've never heard of this minister, but he's one of the associate ministers at Kenneth's dad's church."

"Oh really? Hmm. No wonder he's not familiar. How you holding up, Nai?" Alex asked.

"The truth?"

They both looked at me as they chowed down on their food.

I went on, "It's been kind of rough this past week. As much as I've been there for Kenneth, it just felt like he didn't appreciate it . . . Still doesn't."

"Aw, Nai, you've gotta give him his space. He'll come around," Tanisha said.

"Well, I hope so. I mean, I feel kind of selfish because I personally haven't lost a close relative since my mom passed, so it seems like I don't understand how he's feeling. But at the same time, I want to be there for him," I replied.

"And you can be there for him. Whether you're doing something or you're just sitting there, your presence is appreciated and you gotta know that," Alex said.

"Y'all know me—if this were any other dude I was messing with, I probably wouldn't give two ducks about being around for him." I had to keep in mind that I was in church, so I had to use my selective vocabulary.

"So what was that about earlier in service when he came and got you and made you sit down?" Tanisha asked.

"I honestly was trying to give him space. I didn't think he wanted me to sit with the family."

Alex said, "Girl, you are probably the closest thing to him right now other than his mom. You can't be running away when trouble seems to creep in."

"I didn't consider it running, just staying back." I motioned with my hands.

"The worst thing you can do right now is stay back, Naomi. You've got to stay as close as possible because all he needs is one thirsty female to step up when you step back and it's over," reminded the single Alex.

"Oh y'all know me! I don't play that kinda mess! Don't be trying to school me! Shoot, I'm supposed to school y'all!" I said.

We all laughed. But I knew that my girls were feeding me the right message. Speaking of feeding, I figured it was time to grab my plate before all the food was gone.

I said, "Well, let me go get some food and sit with my man."

"Yeah, you best hurry up before hot mama over there steals your seat," Tanisha said.

I turned to see who she was referring to.

Some thick-legged woman was rapping my Kenneth up with her hand on his shoulder as they stood at the head table next to my reserved seat. I quickly made a detour before getting my plate and went over to introduce myself, but more importantly to find out who this chick was.

I walked up and said, "Well hello, I'm Naomi. And you are?"

I extended my hand for her to shake.

With a faint giggle, she said, "I'm Latasha."

"I'm Kenneth's girlfriend," I blurted out with a fake smile.

She left my hand high and dry and just looked at me.

By now, I know Kenneth had noticed my blood boiling, so he sent Latasha on her way.

"Uh, nice seeing you, Latasha. Thanks again for coming, it means a lot," he said.

"Oh of course. Just keep your head up," she said as she slowly walked away.

My attention quickly diverted to Kenneth as I demanded an explanation with my eyes.

Acting as if nothing had happened, Kenneth said, "Baby, you haven't eaten yet? Come and sit down. There's food here at the head table so you don't have to stand in line."

"Kenneth?!" I stood frozen.

He grabbed my hand and led me to the seat next to his, whispering, "Look, baby, let's not do this now."

"Do what? I just want to know who that chick is. Are you gonna tell me or do I have to ask?"

Quickly, he spit out, "Latasha—she's from my dad's church. A real sweet young lady and there's nothing for you to worry about, honey."

"Then why can't she keep her hands to herself?"

"What? She was consoling me," he responded passively, as if he was trying not to make this a big deal.

"Isn't that what you've got me for?" I asked, feeling insecure.

"Yeah, if you'd stay with me instead of disappearing every few minutes."

He picked up his fork and resumed eating his meal. Meanwhile, I felt like I had just been slapped in the face with his words and I no longer had an appetite. So much for me trying to be there for my boyfriend. I hated to admit it, but Alex was right. I just wished this week would hurry up and be over already.

CHAPTER 46

~TANISHA~

Life was such an amazing thing. It came with so many surprises, disappointments, ups, and even downs. It was the day of my baby shower as we had originally planned. Just a few days ago we were mourning a death and now we were celebrating a new life, my son Joshua. But he was here and I could not complain. Although he was still in the hospital, I thought we should still celebrate him.

Naomi and Alex had so many games set up and some delicious food. And most of all, they still did the gender reveal for me! I loved my best friends.

It was time to wrap things up and for me to give my final remarks.

"You know, God's timing is something else. You all know that Joshua wasn't due for a few more days. The fact that you all still were willing to come out and celebrate with Cameron and me means so much. We're so grateful for all of you. Thanks so much for all the gifts and donations. May God bless you all!"

Everyone clapped.

Cameron stood, as he had one thing to add. "One more thing I believe my wife forgot to mention. I'd call this a praise report. Doctors say that we can bring Josh home on Monday!"

The room was filled with claps and awe.

"I'm sorry! Yes, how could I forget that?!"

Cameron and I hugged one another.

***

After the baby shower, Alex, Naomi, and I decided to spend some girl time together at my place.

Still reeling in joy, I said, "You ladies are honestly the best. Thanks for the shower."

"Oh, it was nothing, girl. We got you," said Alex.

"Yeah, we had too much fun putting that together, didn't we, Alex?" Naomi said.

"YEP!"

"I'm so excited that Josh will be coming home in two days!" Naomi yelled.

She had been drinking all evening. I could tell she needed no more.

"Aren't we all!" I replied.

"Aw, Tan, you get to be on mommy duty for a few weeks," Alex said.

"Yes indeed. But y'all better keep them phones on in case I need y'all!"

"Oh we will, girl!" Naomi said, with her drunk self. "Alex, aren't you starting your training this week?"

"Yeah, I am. A whole month of studying. Then I get ordained."

I asked, "Oh, well then, I guess I can't bug you or ask you to babysit, huh?"

"I wouldn't say that. I can multi-task. Besides, things at work aren't real hectic right now. I've got a little wiggle room," Alex said.

"Y'all, I think I'm getting sleepy," cried Naomi.

I knew she was past her limit.

"Why don't you crash here for a bit, Nai? Until you get yourself together?" I suggested.

"Yeah, I think I'll do that."

I went to get some blankets for her to rest on the couch.

"Looks like somebody won't be making it to church tomorrow." Alex laughed.

I gave Alex the as-if-that's-abnormal look.

"Come on, Nai," I said, trying to guide my friend over to the couch.

She dragged her tired, drunk self onto my couch and my newfound mother instincts began to kick in as I tucked her in.

I knew she was half out of it, but I couldn't help but ask, "Nai, how's Kenneth doing?"

"He's all right, I guess. I haven't been talking to him much," she said in a slur.

"Oh yeah? How come?" Alex asked.

"He acts like he's in his own world. He's distant."

"Hmm, that's not good," I said. "All right then. Good night, Nai."

Naomi threw her hand up, then out she went.

Alex and I remained at the kitchen table but lowered our voices to continue talking.

"Tan, I'm a little worried about Kenneth and her," Alex said.

"Really? I don't think it's that bad."

"You don't? I mean, I know he experienced a loss, so maybe he's grieving. But remember at the funeral when he was talking to that girl? That really got Nai hot and she's been drinking more frequently since then," Alex continued.

"Well, I see what you mean. Did she find out who the girl was?"

"Some chick who goes to his dad's church. But I'm telling you, maybe there's more to the story than what he's telling."

Not wanting to assume, I discarded the idea of Kenneth being unfaithful. "I think Kenneth's a good man. I don't want to believe that he's doing Nai dirty."

"I agree. And lord knows I'm not trying to gossip, but I just look at it as being a concerned friend."

Alex had a point. Naomi was the type of girl to fake like she had it all together even if she didn't. She didn't want people to worry about her and more than anything, she could not stand to be embarrassed.

"You think we should talk to him?" I asked.

"No. Let's just stay out of it unless she asks for our help. Besides, we got our own stuff to deal with."

"You're right," I agreed.

"Well, I'm going to head home and get ready for church tomorrow. Walk me out?" Alex suggested.

"Yeah."

We walked past Naomi, who was knocked out at ten o'clock.

I hugged Alex and thanked her once again for everything. Within the past few months, Alex and I had been through a lot. I wasn't even sure if we would still be friends. But I was glad that we were and that God gave me the strength to forgive my best friend. Most importantly, I was grateful that our friendship had returned to normal.

CHAPTER 47

~ALEXANDRA~

A week into my minister training classes, I found myself overwhelmed with work and studying. I was beginning to question if I could keep up for another three weeks. I had been so busy that I hadn't gotten the chance to visit Tanisha and the baby or even talk to my girls at all the entire week. On my lunch break Friday, I decided to stop at Tanisha's place.

"Aw! He's so cute, Tan! Look at his little chubby cheeks!" I said, pinching Joshua's smiling baby face. He was already so handsome.

Tanisha giggled.

"Girl, he's a mess. He's spoiled already," she said.

"I bet that's your doing, huh?"

"Well yeah. Cam goes to work and I spoil lil' man for eight hours."

"Can I rock him?"

"Sure. He's due for his nap anyhow."

I picked up little seven-pound Joshua and held him in my arms, then joined Tanisha on the couch.

"You know I'm ya auntie, right?" I asked him.

He shot me a slight grin.

Tanisha asked, "So what's been going on with you, Alex?"

"Tanisha, when I tell you I am beat, I mean it. It feels like I'm an undergrad again balancing school and work," I replied tiredly.

"Wow, that's tough. You gonna be able to handle things?"

"Yeah. Work isn't demanding right now, so that's a blessing."

"Ah, that's some relief. I've been working from home for a few hours when I get time in between feedings and Joshua's naps," she said with a yawn.

"So how you been coming along with week one and the baby?" I asked.

"It's good. Just tired, that's all. But I cannot complain," she said, shaking her head.

Joshua was slowly drifting off to sleep in my arms, and God knows I wanted to nap along with him.

She then asked, "Alex, can I share something with you?"

"Anything, Tanisha."

"Cameron and I have decided to go to marriage counseling."

I sat up, somewhat concerned. "Why? Everything's okay, right?"

"Well yeah. But we just want to make sure that we're on the same page. Especially now that Josh is in the picture."

"Does this have anything to do with me?" I was almost afraid to ask, although I was certain that it did. And of course she wouldn't tell me.

"No, no. Trust me, we're not fighting or anything. Just want to keep a lock on things."

Very casually, I responded, "Oh, right."

"Honestly it's something we should have done before we got married. You know, couples don't have to be in a bind to go to counseling."

"Oh, I know. But I'm excited for you. You guys going to Pastor Henderson?"

"Actually we're not sure. We thought about it though."

"Okay. I wish you guys the best." By now Joshua had fallen sound asleep, and I figured it was time to head back to work. "I'm going to go put him in his crib."

"Sure. You want me to fix you a plate to take with you back to work?" Tanisha offered.

"Thanks. I'd appreciate it."

As I walked upstairs to lay Joshua down, I wondered if Tanisha and Cameron were going to counseling because of me or not. I wondered if they were really having problems or going for the sole reason of strengthening their union. All these thoughts began to crowd my mind when, really, it should not have been any of my concern. With all that I had going on, I could not afford any more on my plate. I had to remain focused.

Chapter 48

~Naomi~

I would normally be in church on most Sunday mornings, but this particular Sunday, I stayed home because I was hung over. I couldn't keep up with how much I had been drinking this past week. I woke up around noon, grabbed myself a bottle of water, and then crawled back into my bed. Glancing at my cell phone, I saw that Alex had texted me a few hours ago.

"WHERE ARE YOU?"

She was probably looking for me in Sunday school. By now, I was sure that the preacher was up delivering the message. I responded, "AT HOME. HUNG OVER."

I turned on the television. Of course nothing was on.

My phone rang and the caller ID flashed Kenneth's name. I really didn't want to talk to him, but I picked up anyway.

I answered in a not-so-welcoming voice, "Hello?"

"Somebody sounds groggy. What's up with that?"

"I just woke up," I replied.

"This late? Why aren't you in church? I was sure you wouldn't answer."

"I'm clearly not there. I'm tired."

"What's wrong? Why you giving me attitude?" he asked.

I knew he could feel my negative energy through the phone.

"Because I'm watching Joel Osteen."

He had to know I was lying. I couldn't watch preacher shows.

"Since when? Now I know you lying. You just don't wanna talk to me."

I remained silent.

He said, "Hello?"

"What?" I said like a whining child.

"Where is my girlfriend? I don't like this new Naomi."

I said, "I'm about to hop in the shower. I'll call you back."

Click.

I didn't mean to be rude but if only Kenneth understood how I'd felt about him within the last two weeks. His attitude was ugly and I didn't appreciate it. I eventually got up and took a shower. When I got out, I fixed myself brunch. By now, it was a little after one. That's when my doorbell rang, and I just knew it was Alex paying me a visit since I didn't come to church. I opened the door to see Kenneth standing there.

He asked, "Uh, can I come in?"

"Sure," I said in a dry tone, walking away.

"Baby, what's wrong? You haven't been acting like yourself." He closed the door behind him.

Kenneth wasn't a mind reader, so I figured I'd stop holding in what I was feeling. "Kenneth, do you love me?"

"What? Of course I do. Why are you asking me that?"

We sat on the couch and I began spilling it all out.

"I haven't been getting that feeling lately. I know you've been dealing with a lot and I don't want to sound selfish. I just miss you and want you back to normal."

He responded, "Normal? Naomi, I'm okay. Things were a little tough these last few weeks."

"I was trying to be there for you, but you felt so distant. And then when I saw that girl from your dad's church, I got a bad feeling," I finally admitted.

"Feeling? Like I'm into her or something?"

"Yes," I said with a straight, pouty face.

Kenneth laughed. I failed to understand what was funny. I could admit that I had a reputation for being a brat, which is one of the reasons why many guys didn't stick around. And Kenneth putting up with my brattiness was not okay, but he and I both knew that I was a work in progress. And so, here we were taking things one day at a time.

"Nai, I've known that girl for years. Not once have we had anything going on. Besides, I got you. Why would I be interested in anyone else?"

"I don't know, Kenneth, that's the thing. I felt like I was being pushed away and when I saw her, my brain just went left."

He then kissed me slowly on the lips.

"I'm sorry that you had those feelings, baby. But trust me, you're more than enough for me," he said with assurance.

With the death of his father being the hot topic for two weeks, sex had definitely not been on our minds. Now that Kenneth was returning to his usual self, his kiss reminded me how much I had missed him.

"Babe, I'm sorry for tripping over something so stupid," I said.

"And you're sorry for accusing me of dealing with another woman?"

"Mmhmm."

Apparently he was hot and horny and couldn't keep his lips to himself. I thought, *Oh how I missed my man!*

CHAPTER 49

~TANISHA~

Cameron and I were a week into our marriage counseling with the pastor. It felt slightly odd at first, but I was beginning to become comfortable being verbal and transparent with my husband.

"When I first met Cameron, I didn't think that we would hit it off. We were so different and I really didn't have time for a relationship. But he kept trying and that was attractive to me."

"You see, it's always when we least expect God to move us and when we seem to make excuses that He places direct people in our lives," Pastor Henderson said.

"You're right," Cameron said. "I knew in my spirit that Tanisha was who He called to be my wife."

"And from the point you two exchanged vows, life has been sweet, huh?" Pastor Henderson asked.

"Of course," Cameron replied, a little too quickly, I thought.

Pastor Henderson said, "Well, amen to that! Would you agree to that, Tanisha?"

I felt it was time for the pastor to know about Cameron's infidelity. I mean, we were in counseling and it was all or nothing.

"Not exactly, Pastor," I said.

Cameron's eyebrows rose.

"Oh? What does that mean?" Pastor Henderson inquired.

"Babe, now?" Cameron asked.

I whispered, "It's now or never." I knew he wasn't happy about it, but I wanted to say it.

"Um, a few months ago Cameron and I were at odds. He—"

"I cheated," Cameron said. I turned and looked at him and could see the hurt and defeat in his face. He looked at me and said, "You happy? Because that's what you wanted to get off your chest, huh?"

He then got up, grabbed the car seat with our son in it, and walked out the door as the pastor sat up at his desk.

"Excuse me, Pastor." I ran out the door behind my husband and picked up a light jog as I tried to catch up with Cameron.

"Cam?!"

He stopped and faced me. "So that's why you wanted to come to counseling? To let it all out so you could feel better? I thought we wiped our hands clean of this, Tan."

"Baby, we have. And that's not why I wanted to come to counseling," I lied.

"Then what was that?!"

This was the first time I had seen my husband enraged since we'd been married.

On the verge of tears, I replied, "If we are going to be open with anybody about us, then it should be Pastor Henderson! Cameron, you know I'm not doing this to hurt you."

"Then why bring this back up? I mean, it's like you're still holding onto it or something. I'm confused."

"Baby, I'm not holding onto it. I just think that if we are open, we can fully heal and thrive with this counseling."

With disappointment in his voice, he said, "Heal? So you're *not* over it."

I couldn't believe he was sitting here picking a fight with me in the church hallway as if running out of the pastor's office wasn't embarrassing enough. Thankfully it wasn't Sunday.

"We'll be in the car waiting." Cameron walked off with Joshua.

I stood there feeling like I was all alone once again. How could Cameron be upset with me for something that he caused? Maybe I wasn't fully over the situation. But I had every right to bring it up to my pastor, someone I could trust to be a lending, confidential ear and spiritual beam of advice. I leaned against the wall, then slid to the ground in the comfort of my own arms, releasing tears that could not be held back any longer.

CHAPTER 50

~ALEXANDRA~

I was in study mode the entire week, but as usual, I found myself taking multiple breaks. Things at work had slowed down, so I spent most of my time studying at the office. Snacking on a bag of chips, I thought about Naomi and what she was up to. I hadn't heard from her in almost two weeks, so I picked up the phone and called her.

"Girl, where you been?!"

"You know where to find me, Alex! I'm at work right now. What's going on?" she asked.

"I figured. You got a minute?"

"Of course. I'm not doing much anyhow at this place. Girl, I'm so ready to get off. These geriatrics are getting on my last nerve!"

"Don't say that, Nai. You better be grateful!"

"The Lord knows my heart. What's been going on with you? I got five minutes before I have to administer some more medicine."

"Sitting here studying at my desk for my training."

"Alex, I'm so proud of you for going through with this. This is life-changing!"

"Don't I know it? How are you and Kenneth?" I asked out of curiosity but more so concern.

She quickly answered, "We're fine."

"Oh yeah? Last I heard y'all weren't talking much. But I guess that was like a few weeks ago."

"Yeah, chile. You know we made up by now!" Naomi said happily.

She could've fooled me.

"Oh yeah? I mean, I don't know. You made it seem like things were terrible."

I had a bad habit of being nosy.

Naomi said, "I'm just a big baby, Alex! We talked things over and smashed—I mean, hashed some things out!"

I started laughing.

"You know what, Nai, you are a mess!"

"How's Tanisha and the baby? I feel like I haven't spoken to her lately either. Girl, I've been off the radar trying to get this promotion and everything."

"She's cool. She and Cameron have taken up marriage counseling," I said, spilling the tea.

"Uh, counseling? For what?"

"She swears it's just to strengthen their marriage."

"And you believe otherwise?" she asked.

"Kind of."

Naomi knew me and she knew that if I was bringing up some tea, then I had concerns. But she knew how to keep me on track and reel me back in.

"Well, don't trip, girl. If she says that's why, then that's why. Just leave it at that."

"You're right. Like I told myself, I don't have time to be focusing on anything that's distracting. I've got a goal to achieve," I reminded myself.

"Amen to that! Well, you know I'd love to keep talking but let me get on back to business. We'll talk later though."

"Okay then. Later, Nai."

She was right. I needed to stop thinking so heavily on something that was behind me. However, my conscience wouldn't let me do that so easily. I picked up the phone to dial Tanisha, but then Taki, my assistant, buzzed in.

"Ms. Moore, there's a call waiting for you on line two. It's urgent," she said.

I put down my cell and picked up the office line with a sigh.

"Ms. Moore speaking . . . "

CHAPTER 51

~NAOMI~

Kenneth and I had arranged dinner plans at a new restaurant downtown, and I was meeting him there after work.

After pulling into what seemed to be a faraway parking space, I got a call from Leon. What bad timing this guy seemed to have. What the heck did he want?

I answered while grabbing my things. "Hi Leon."

"Hey Naomi, you busy?"

"Actually yeah. I'm about to walk into dinner with my boyfriend. Everything okay?"

"Oh, yeah. I'm good. Well, don't let me hold you up. We can talk another time."

"You sure?"

"Yeah, have a good evening," he said.

"Okay. Bye." I hung up.

Whatever it was would have to wait until later. I was hungry and already running a bit late.

I found Kenneth waiting for me outside the restaurant.

He said, "Hey baby, you look gorgeous."

"Oh please, it's just my after-work clothes," I said passively.

"But it's you in them. You are beautiful." He leaned in for a kiss.

We entered the restaurant and apparently he had made a reservation because we didn't have to wait like all the others in the waiting area.

Amazed at the decor, I said, "Wow, Kenneth, this place is nice! It's been here about what, two months now?"

"Yep. It has a nice ambiance to it. I'm enjoying these dim lights," he said in a freaky tone.

"Baby, when is the last time we did something special?" I asked.

"Uh, I think when we went to the aquarium and your friend Tanisha hit you up 'cause she was at the hospital."

Did he have a good memory or what? We didn't get out much, but whenever we did it was always something to be amazed by.

"Oh yeah. That was a long time ago. But aren't you glad we are out?"

"Of course I am. We need to do this more often," Kenneth said.

Our server walked up to our table and Kenneth ordered a bottle of wine. I knew what that meant for us tonight . . .

Over dinner, Kenneth began to talk a lot about the future. He discussed how things were looking up for him at the accounting firm, and I shared how I was considering a potential promotion in the medical field.

"Life is moving, Naomi. We've got to make sure we keep up, right?"

"Oh yes, I'm not going anywhere. I hope you aren't. Do you want kids, baby?"

He laughed. "Eventually, when we get married."

This was our first time discussing serious business relating to our relationship. It was good to know that Kenneth was traditional like me and preferred to be married before having children.

I took a sip of wine. "And when will that be? I'm ready!" I responded, throwing my hands in the air. I was starting to feel loose.

Kenneth smiled.

"When the time is right, baby, we will know," he said with a sly grin.

CHAPTER 52

~TANISHA~

I had left our last counseling session embarrassed by the disagreement with Cameron. Once again, our marriage was in a tight spot. I did not enjoy putting on a front to my husband but living a lie was not the ideal thing to do either. Consequently, I showed up this time alone. I was somewhat excited to speak to Pastor Henderson because there was not much conversation going on at home.

"Pastor, let me just start by saying that I am truly sorry about what happened at our last session. I had no idea that this would upset Cameron so much," I said.

"Tanisha, you don't have to apologize to me. I understand these kinds of things. I just want to help you two heal from your situation but first, you must be honest with yourselves. Is this the reason you came for counseling?"

I took a deep breath.

"I thought I moved on from this but honestly I don't think that I have. Which leads me to believe that I suckered Cameron into coming."

Pastor Henderson said, "All right then. You are being honest. Have you forgiven your husband for what he did?"

"Yes, I have. I just haven't forgotten."

"You may never forget, Tanisha. But if you fail to bury the memory of what he did to you, then you will forever hold a bit of hatred in your heart. You know in Colossians chapter three, we are told to forgive as our father has forgiven us and to rid ourselves of anger and other things. Do not harbor anger in your heart if you already forgave Cameron."

Pastor was hitting the nail on the head.

"But how can I forget? I want to forget but it's hard," I cried.

"Pray to the Lord to deliver your thoughts from that place and be patient about it. Meanwhile, love your husband regardless. You know Cameron loves you," Pastor said with a gentle smile.

I knew Cameron loved me and that all he did was make a mistake. I quickly realized that I could not hold a grudge against him. If I had been the one who messed up, Cam would have the strength to forgive me. And as much as God forgives us, I owed it to my husband to do God's will and forgive him.

Pastor Henderson delivered a quick prayer and gave me some resources that Cameron and I could use to work through our situation together. Counseling was not over for us, but getting this burden off my chest with some help was the start of things getting better. I could not wait to get home and begin communicating more with Cameron.

I stood to shake his hand and said, "Thank you so much, Pastor. I have no idea why I did not come to you when this first took place."

"Mmm, perhaps you were afraid. All that matters, Tanisha, is that you and Cameron are taking one step at a time and in this together."

"Yeah, together," I echoed.

CHAPTER 53

~ALEXANDRA~

After things at work slowly began to pick back up, so did the intensity of my minister training. But I remained persistent as it was almost time for my ordination.

"Oh em gee! These ribs are AMAZING!" I hollered out.

It had been so long since I'd gotten my hands on some good old soul food. Tanisha and I met for a late lunch at Detroit Soul, one of the best places in town.

"Mmhmm, and I sure brought my appetite!" Tanisha said with a mouthful.

"How's counseling going?" I just blurted it out.

"Well, it's been okay for the most part."

"Oh yeah? What went wrong?"

"Uh you know, it's just something new, so it's slightly uncomfortable for Cameron."

I could tell by her vibe that she wasn't being straightforward.

I asked, "Tan, what really happened?" as I continued delving into my rib platter.

"Well, I brought up Cameron's past."

"His past as in before you came along?"

She rolled her eyes and finally decided to just let it out.

"No, Cameron cheating on me!"

My eyes grew wide. "YOU WHAT?!" I knew it. But I needed to keep my cool, so I took a deep breath and turned my voice down. Luckily we had a corner booth. "Tan, you told Pastor about me and him?" I whispered.

"Of course not! I wouldn't go that far!" Tanisha snapped back.

"So are you telling me that's your *real* reason for going to counseling?"

"Huh? Well, you see, at first it wasn't. But when we started opening up, I felt like I should free myself of everything," Tanisha said, wiping her mouth of the excessive barbeque sauce.

Everything, huh? I didn't know if I was hurt by all of this or happy for her getting what she needed. Apparently this situation was not a thing of the past for her.

"I thought you freed yourself months ago and buried all of that," I said.

"Okay, well, apparently I didn't, Alex. Why are you sweating me?"

"Oh I'm not. I'm just going by what you tell me. How did Cameron take it?"

"How do you think he took it?!" Tanisha raised her voice.

It was evident that this conversation was beginning to go left. I wiped my hands and put my ribs on hold so that I could give my full attention to my best friend.

"Look, Tanisha, I've apologized once and I hate to think that you need me to apologize again."

"I'm not looking for anything from you, Alex. I'm getting what I need from this counseling with Pastor

Henderson. Does that bother you? Because it seems like it does."

I didn't want or expect things to go this way. The last thing I wanted to do was argue with my best friend about things that took place in our past. But she was right. I thought I gave her all the time she needed to completely heal from the situation but maybe she needed more time and guidance.

"I'm sorry, Tanisha. I should've never asked," I said.

CHAPTER 54

~NAOMI~

"Babe, I'll call you when I get a break from work. Love you." With no time for breakfast or even a quickie, Kenneth quickly grabbed his things and headed for the door.

I was so mad that he had been called in to work on a Saturday. Luckily we didn't have any plans.

Since our date, Kenneth and I had found ourselves happier than ever. I was still in shock that we had even lasted this long! Usually I was known to be a hit-it-and-quit-it type of girl, but Kenneth was showing me things I had never seen before with anyone else.

Still in bed while scrolling through my text messages, I came across Leon's thread. I suddenly remembered he had called me the other night before my dinner date and seemed to have something on his mind. So I called him.

"Hey Leon, is this a good time?"

"Oh sure. What's up?"

"I'm actually returning your call from the other night. How's everything?"

"Oh you know, everything is everything. But I called to see if you could do a favor for your boy."

Favors? I wasn't into doing favors for people unless it was beneficial to me. And what kind of favor could he want from me?

I asked with a laugh, "Um, what's that?"

"Talk to your girl Alex for me."

With a complementary eye roll, I asked, "About?"

"Going out with me."

"Leon, come on. How many times have we been through this? We are not little kids!"

"Please? Just one date?" he whined.

This dude had tried so many times to get with Alex over the past few years, and she had made it clear that she had no intention of being anything other than friends, if that. I was about sick of him and his antics.

"No Leon, I can't do that. You know she's not into you."

"She doesn't know if she doesn't give it a shot," he said confidently.

Sometimes I thought Leon forgot that he was married and had a family. I knew his marriage was a bit shaky but this was too much.

"Look, don't you have her number? Call her yourself!"

"She won't answer."

By now, he was asking for a curse out, so I snapped him back into reality.

"Leon, what is going on with you? I returned your call because I was under the impression that you had some type of emergency going on, but it's just the same old mess once again. You do know that you're married, right? Or have you forgotten that fast?!"

Silence grew on the other line.

"Hello?!" I hollered.

"We've decided to get a divorce."

I took a deep gasp. "Wow. I'm so sorry."

"Oh, don't be. I think we both knew that this was an option soon as opposed to later." He seemed to be okay with it all.

Now I understood why Leon kept pressing to get with Alex. I thought he was just taking a joke too far.

"Are you okay with the decision?" I asked carefully.

"Of course. I basically have no choice. It was one of those things where you know it's broke and can't be fixed, so trying isn't even an option. Just throw the whole thing away," he said with a slight, passive laugh.

"But still, don't you think it's a bit hasty to talk to Alex?"

"Naomi, I'm not getting any younger."

That statement alone reminded me that Leon was a bit older than all three of us, and it also reminded me that I was getting older as well, which led me to think about my future timeline and if I was on the right track with Kenneth.

I went on, "Okay, but you have two kids to think about. Why rush them into something they have no clue about? Don't you need time to heal? I mean, you two probably haven't even put the ink on the papers yet and you're already exploring other options!"

"Naomi, when you know what you want, you go for it. Honestly, part of me feels that I should've never stepped into this marriage to begin with but I did. I saw the signs but I chose to accept her regardless. But I'm not going to sit here and feel sorry for myself. I have to move on."

All I could do was shake my head on the other end of that phone. It was all too much and so sudden. I felt like I was in middle school, passing a "will you date me?" handwritten note, relaying messages back and forth between my friend and colleague. Leon was in no position to give up his fight but I already knew Alex's answer, and a divorce wasn't going to change it.

CHAPTER 55

~TANISHA~

It had been a month post counseling and I was happy that things at home with Cameron had gotten better. We realized that our family was in a good place and that our lack of trust in one another had to cease for the sake of our son. I had no doubt that Cameron and I were meant to be together. One slipup was enough for me to worry but it wasn't going to be enough to end my marriage.

As I sat at the kitchen table feeding Joshua and trying to pay some bills, in walked my chocolate hubby from work.

"Hey, baby, how's everything?" he said, planting a kiss on my cheek.

"Oh you know, the usual. Me attempting to do bills but your son won't cooperate," I said.

"Here, let me handle that."

He took Joshua in his arms and began to feed him his bottle. It was so much work taking care of my son but also trying to take care of all of us! As much as I tried to play it off, Cameron knew me. He knew that I was a tired mess, but I loved how he stepped up as my husband.

Focusing my attention on him, I asked, "Babe, how was work? I've got some dinner in the oven for you."

"Aw, thanks, hon. Work was long and boring once again. But I'm glad to be home with my two favorite people."

I smiled. "Well, in a few weeks I'll be back in the long and boring hassle myself," I said with no excitement.

"Oh that's right. You up for it?" Cameron asked.

"Maybe I will be when it's time. For now, I'm soaking up all my freedom from the office and telework," I said while stretching.

I was not looking forward to going back to work. I wanted to remain at home with my son. The thought of placing him in daycare scared me.

"You know what I was thinking, baby?" Cameron asked.

"What's that?"

"How about when you get some time off again, we take a little mini vacay? Just the two of us, huh?"

"Aw, babe, isn't it too soon? I mean, Josh is only a few months old and I don't want to think about being away from him for so long just yet."

"Well, that's the thing, neither do I. But maybe we can actually plan something in advance months from now. You deserve some relaxation, and that's not up for discussion."

Cameron's face was so serious. How could a woman argue with a man who knew just what she needed?

"All right, babe, whatever you say," I responded to my king.

"I have another suggestion for you."

"Sure, babe, what?"

"How about I put Josh down for a nap, and when you're done with what you're doing, you meet me in the bedroom?"

Recently, Cameron and I had been having the most intimacy we'd ever had since knowing one another. It was as if we were two horny teenagers who'd just discovered sex. But it was amazing and I definitely was not complaining.

Very amused with his idea, I quickly closed my laptop and figured I could come back and finish the bills later.

"I'll see you when you get there," I said, making my way up the stairs while seducing him with my eyes.

CHAPTER 56

~ALEXANDRA~

The time had come. All the late-night studying, sleepless nights, and stressful days were finally coming to an end. I was about to become a minister. My mom and siblings were in attendance as well as my friends of course—all the support I needed. Lucky for me I was not the only candidate being licensed, which helped take some of the pressure off of me. An older lady from the church, Sister Carey, had also been studying to become a minister. I was so nervous sitting in Pastor Henderson's office.

"Alex, I know you're nervous but if it helps so am I," Sister Carey said.

"How could you not be nervous?" I responded with a chuckle. "I mean, I'm ready. Just anxious, that's all."

"Oh trust me, I know. I'm forty and I'm still a little shocked that God has called me at this season in my life to start preaching. I never questioned Him though because I know this is His purpose for me," she said confidently.

Pastor Henderson entered the office along with two of the deacons.

"All right, my beloved sisters. Are we ready to go?"

"Yes, Pastor. I'm as ready as I will ever be," I replied strongly.

We said a prayer and proceeded to the front doors of the sanctuary. I felt like I had just finished running a marathon the way my heart was jumping. I looked at Sister Carey and she gave me that motherly grin as if to say, *You got this.*

***

What felt like forever was only an hour according to my watch.

As Pastor Henderson was giving remarks before pronouncing us as ministers, my mind blurred out of my present surroundings and I sat there thinking about my life. Here I was, only twenty-six years young and becoming something that not many people my age look forward to becoming. I thought about my past, where and how I had been brought up. Not having a present father in my life because drugs were more important to him. Watching my mother struggle yet nurture her children into intelligent somebodies. Somehow I failed to succumb to all the labels and those who believed in me to fail. Who would've thought?

"Church family, I now present to you Minister Aileen Carey and Minister Alexandra Moore!"

I quickly snapped back into reality as the congregation stood and clapped for us. Almost immediately, the tears began to fall and I leaned my head back and thanked the Lord for this undeserved opportunity.

After the ordination service, refreshments were served in the church's banquet hall. But before meeting and greeting everyone, Pastor Henderson called Sister Carey and me into his office once again.

"Sisters, or should I rightfully say Ministers, let me quickly express to you both how proud I am of you. I thanked God when he placed you two in my spirit to be ordained. But I thank him now for getting you through this process as I know it was not easy. Just let me remind you that your dedication to Him and His work is just as important as the job itself. God bless you both. Now, don't let me hold you any longer. I shall see you two Sunday morning."

I leaned in for a hug. "Thank you, Pastor!"

Sister Carey and I looked at one another and hugged.

"God bless you, sista!" I said.

"And God bless you, Alex."

We joined everyone in the banquet hall, and as much as I wanted to get to the good-smelling food, I knew I had to hug and kiss everyone as they gave their congratulations.

My mom, with tears in her eyes, said, "Oh Alex, I'm so proud of you! I'm so happy for you!"

"Thanks, Mom. I love you."

I hugged my younger siblings, who expressed their excitement for me as well.

After taking endless pictures I finally got to sit down and eat with my girls and family.

"Alex, did I tell you how well you aced those questions, girl? You left Sister Carey in the dust, chile," Naomi said.

"Naomi, stop it!" I laughed.

"You know I'm just kidding. Y'all killed it! My best friend is a minister now! Don't be judging my chameleon Christian-self neither."

"I'm in no position to judge you or anybody else, Nai."

"I never saw this day coming, Alex. You make me so proud!" Tanisha squealed as she hugged me.

"Thanks, ladies. I couldn't have done it without your support," I said.

"So hold up, if I can't make it to church because I'm hungover or something, does that mean you can come over and serve me my communion?" Naomi asked.

"Girl, BYE!" I replied.

CHAPTER 57

~NAOMI~

A week after Alex's ordination ceremony, Kenneth rushed home after work with some exciting news: He got a promotion at his job! Things were really looking up for us. If only *my* life had the potential to promote itself.

It was Saturday night and I had been doing household chores all day. I decided to take a nap before I headed to dinner that night. Kenneth had invited me out for a night on the town and told me to look "cute." As if I didn't do that already. When I woke up from my nap, I picked out my outfit.

Now does he want me to be dressy dressy or just dressy? I thought.

I decided to go with my black jumpsuit and red heels. You could never go wrong with all black.

He told me to be ready at six o'clock, and it was exactly that time when my doorbell rang.

I grabbed my jacket and opened the door.

Kenneth, caught by surprise, said, "Well, damn, baby! I wasn't expecting this!"

"What?! Am I too much or not enough?!"

"You are more than enough, baby," he said, taking hold of my hand.

As we proceeded to the car, I became curious about where Kenneth was taking me. He opened my car door and I jumped in like it was my high school prom night. When he got in, I asked him to drop a hint about where we were headed.

"Uh, it's about thirty minutes away. Just relax, babe," he said.

Thirty minutes?! Although that sounded like a long time, it really wasn't that bad. At least I knew he wasn't taking me to some old fast-food joint down the street because the only places in my neighborhood were rugged, worn-down establishments.

Approximately thirty minutes later, we arrived at an Italian restaurant, so fancy that I couldn't even pronounce the name.

"Here we are, baby. Let me get your door." Kenneth jumped out of the car.

I loved the way Kenneth treated me like a queen.

For some reason, I was nervous upon entering this restaurant. I wondered why Kenneth was doing this—to celebrate his promotion? To celebrate us? Just because? Whatever the case, I didn't bother to ask because there didn't have to be a special occasion for us to go out. Besides, I was used to going out to eat a lot lately, mainly because I was too tired to cook after work.

We walked into the restaurant and the hostess greeted us with a smile.

"Hello! How are you two today?"

Kenneth spoke up. "We're doing awesome. I believe there is a reservation listed under Kenneth Myers."

The hostess scanned her chart. Then she gave my man a coquettish look. I quickly glanced at Kenneth, who had a smirk on his face along with a raised eyebrow.

"Oh yes! Right this way!" she squealed.

We followed the hostess and I whispered to Kenneth, "Is there something I should know about? What was that?!"

"Baby, just chill. We're almost there."

Almost there? What did he mean?

I forwarded my attention to what was in front of me, and looking beyond the hostess' head, I caught a glance of Tanisha holding Joshua in her arms. And there was more to see.

My jaw dropped when I saw Cameron along with Alex and a few other mutual friends of ours.

The hostess dropped us off and I ran and hugged my girls, all while asking, "What are y'all doing here?!" and checking out their outfits and noticing that they, too, were all dressed up.

I slowly turned around and there was Kenneth on bended knee.

I swore I was in a dream.

"Naomi, I knew from the day I met you that we were meant to be. I love you; I tell you all the time and I really mean it. I'm not a guy of many words but you are something special to me. We've taken the time to know one another and I'm already convinced that you're perfect. You're beautiful, smart, funny, and most importantly, you love me for me. I can only ask one thing of you."

Kenneth pulled a tiny box from behind his back and opened it.

"Will you marry me?" he asked with his deep, sexy voice.

By now, we had attracted the attention of the nearby patrons. I was crying floods of tears and I was so choked up that it took a pat on the back from Alex to slap me back into reality.

"YES! YES, KENNETH!"

He got up and everyone clapped and shared in the excitement. Kenneth placed the ring on my finger and we kissed before I buried my face full of tears into his chest.

After all the hugs and congrats, we all sat down to enjoy a delicious meal. Meanwhile, I was basking in this moment. For the life of me, I could not believe that I was engaged! Kenneth was very important to me. For the past year I had dedicated my life to this man and placed the hoe that I was into the trash where she belonged! I did not say yes because he was the first ever to propose to me; I said yes because I knew deep down that Kenneth really was beneficial to me. He treated me like a queen, supported my dreams, and most of all, he loved me! I couldn't be happier! I could see my future with him unlike all the others in my past.

As dinner had almost come to an end, my girls and I retreated to the outside balcony with our champagne glasses.

"Nai, I'm excited for you!" Tanisha said.

"Just think, now you have a wedding to plan!" Alex chimed in.

I said, "Yes ladies, WE have yet another wedding to plan! Tan, you know I'ma need some help!"

"I gotchu!" Tanisha said.

"Y'all, I was not expecting this AT ALL! I'm so mad that y'all did not tell me! At least drop a clue or something!"

Tanisha said, "Girl, now why would we do that? To ruin it?"

"Right. Besides, with all that minister training in effect, it really slipped my mind," Alex said.

"Wait, so y'all knew about this?" I asked, pointing my finger at the both of them.

"Yeah. Tan told me about it," Alex said, only to get herself off the hook.

Tanisha said with a smile, "I only knew because Kenneth mentioned it to Cameron, who mentioned it to me. Then he asked if he was making the right decision. We all know how you feel about him, so it was a definite yes!"

"Ooooh, I'ma get y'all!" I said.

I loved my girls. Throughout the years that we'd known each other, we'd been to hell and back together. And sometimes, we literally fought like sisters. But one thing never changed: we always had each other's backs.

"Group hug!" Alex yelled.

The three of us hugged. I was basking in this moment and didn't want to let go.

"Now let's get back in here so I can get my dessert!" I said.

"You are talking about food, right?" Tanisha asked.

"Of course! What else could I be referring to?" I replied seductively.

"Y'all might be engaged but don't make me pull out the anointing oil!" Alex teased.

We all laughed as we retreated inside.

CPSIA information can be obtained
at www.ICGtesting.com
Printed in the USA
LVHW030200220122
708928LV00003B/61